SLEEP-OVER TAKE-OVER

SIMON JAMES GREEN

ILLUSTRATED BY ALEKSEI BITSKOFF

SCHOLASTIC

Published in the UK by Scholastic, 2022
Euston House, 24 Eversholt Street, London, NW1 1DB, UK
Scholastic Ireland, 89E Lagan Road, Dublin Industrial Estate, Glasnevin,
Dublin, D11 HP5F

Text © Simon James Green, 2022
Illustrations © Aleksei Bitskoff, 2022

ISBN 978 0702 30363 0

A CIP catalogue record for this book
is available from the British Library.

Printed by CPI Group (UK) Ltd, Croydon, CR0 4YY
Paper made from wood grown in sustainable forests
and other controlled sources.

1 3 5 7 9 10 8 6 4 2

www.scholastic.co.uk

SLEEP-
OVER
TAKE-
OVER

700042880665

For Jacqui Sydney and year 5 & 6 at
Old Buckenham Primary School
&
Angela Kent and year 5 & 6 at
Four Lanes Junior School

CHAPTER 1
A PERFECTLY FINE PLAN

Looking back, we probably should just have stuck to the plan. If we'd stuck to the plan, none of the bad stuff would have happened. Although, it is also true that none of the good stuff would have happened either. Funny, isn't it, how so much can change, just because of one simple thing that you do?

Anyway, as weekend plans went, things were shaping up quite nicely. For a start, it was already Friday – and who doesn't love a Friday? Two days of freedom stretching out in front of you? Perfect! This was a slightly different Friday to normal, though, because our regular teacher, Miss Percival, had been given the day off so she could prepare for her BIG WEDDING on Sunday. Miss Percival had been ~~going on~~ telling us about her wedding ~~for ten long years~~ since the start of term, showing us pictures of her wedding cake, and asking if we thought she should go with a purple-and-silver or red-and-gold theme for the table decorations. Personally, both options sounded a little gaudy, and I might have gone with an elegant mix of cream and peach; but, to be fair, her wedding sounded like it would be amazing. I overheard Mum talking on the phone, and apparently Miss Percival was going to her wedding as "Bridezilla". I think it's really cool that Miss Percival is having a Godzilla-themed wedding, and she's going as a destructive, prehistoric sea monster. She's my favourite teacher ever for a good reason, and I bet the wedding will be really memorable.

With Miss Percival busy getting her monster outfit ready, it meant our head teacher, Mr Banerjee, was in charge of our class. Mr Banerjee used to be in the army, and loves nothing more than teaching us survival techniques, which may or may not be connected to the fact we're all due to start secondary school later this year.

"SCENARIO!" Mr Banerjee barked as he strolled around our classroom in his favourite (if somewhat unconventional for a teacher) camouflage outfit. "You're lost in enemy territory. It's dark. There's a storm. There's been a sighting of a wild beast – possibly some kind of mutant wolf escaped from a lab." Mr Banerjee bent down to our table, getting right up close to my best mate Jagger's ear, which was almost invisible under his chaotic hair that made it look like he'd just rolled out of bed. Jagger's parents are originally from South Korea, but he tends not to tell people that because their next question is often about K-Pop, and despite the fact Jagger's mum named him after her favourite singer from a band called the Rolling Stones, Jagger is not interested in music or singing. Funny story: he recently lost a bet with me about how long it's possible to wear the same pair of underpants before your mum or dad gets suspicious (eight days – go me!) and his dare was to send an audition tape to the Barbara Scarborough

School of Performing Arts. I heard his song. Truly horrendous. No wonder he doesn't like music – the kid's tone-deaf. Unsurprisingly, he didn't hear back from them.

"Mr Jung?" Mr Banerjee said to Jagger (he likes calling us by our last names). "What do you do first?"

"Find food – preferably some kind of fried chicken. Fries, nice side of gravy – maybe some beans."

"WRONG!" Mr Banerjee shouted. "Food is not a priority. It's possible to survive for three *weeks* without food!"

I raised my eyebrow at Jagger. I knew for a fact he couldn't last three *hours* without a Laughing Cow cheese triangle and a bag of Skittles. And yes, he did eat them together because he's weird like that.

"Mr Bumble!" Mr Banerjee said, pointing at me. *"What would you do first?* Come on! You're lost! Escaped werewolf! What would you do?"

I took a deep breath, considering my options. "Honestly, sir, I think I'd probably just lay down and let the mutant werewolf find me and eat me. I reckon it'd be easier that way and—"

"He's just an eleven-year-old boy," Jagger added.

"Exactly!" I said.

"And a short one at that," Jack Jones, the football captain chipped in, like that was a punchline to a joke, rather than just a statement of fact.

I shrugged. I *was* short. According to our recent "Healthy Bodies" class (the content of which made me feel quite sick, to be honest with you), at some point in the next three years, I would probably grow; but in the meantime, I was fine with short. Jagger was pretty short too. We could be short *together*.

"Mutant werewolf versus *short* eleven-year-old boy? I don't think so, sir," I said. "I think that would be game over. Finito! The End! Terminated—"

"Find shelter, Bumble!" Mr Banerjee barked. "Just find shelter! That's what you do!"

"Find shelter, BUM-ble!" Jack Jones repeated, to appreciative laughter from the rest of his footie mates, like they'd never heard that joke before.

I bowed my head and sighed.

Jagger nudged my leg with his under the desk. That was him telling me it'd be OK, he'd got my back, and just to ignore Jack. Which is why Jagger took the attention away from me, like he often did, by playing the clown. "Ooh!" he said. "Find shelter? Like the kids who find that gingerbread house in that fairy tale!" Jagger frowned. "Oh, wait, wasn't that a witch in the end, though? What if the shelter belongs to a witch, sir? Should we still go in?"

Mr Banerjee was glaring at Jagger. "No! Obviously don't go into a witch's house! Not that ... argh! Witches aren't real!"

There were murmurs of discontent among the class. If witches weren't real, why were there so many books written about them? And there were definitely more witch books than books about mutant werewolves – which apparently *were* real.

"But, sir! There's a witch that lives near Otis."

I nodded. "True! She has a garden full of gnomes!"

"How does that make her a witch?" Mr Banerjee asked.

"Because they were once regular kids who she turned to stone with her witchy powers," I told him. "They say that every time a kid leaves town, a new gnome appears, which begs the question – *did the kid really leave town?*"

There was a groan from behind me and someone on the "Drama Darlings" table (probably Kyle Benson because he has *no* sense of humour) muttered, "Please be quiet."

"I can't help the story!" I said.

"Otis can't help the story!" Jagger added, by way of back-up.

"This is not about going into a stranger's house!" Mr Banerjee said. "You make your own!"

"Our own house?" I said. "How? We'd have to draw up plans … get the materials… I can't lay bricks, or wire up electrics!"

"Should we wire our own electrics, sir?" Jagger asked. "Should we plug directly into the national grid? I hear if you wear wellies, you can insulate yourself against electric shocks?"

"You build a simple shelter out of fallen branches, twigs, leaves – anything you can get your hands on," Mr Banerjee said, patiently. He must have seen the look of doubt on my face, because he then added, "What is it, Mr Bumble?"

"Mmmm," I said, chewing my lip a bit. "It's just, my dad tried to build an extension to our house himself, and the council refused planning approval and made him tear it down because it was built with the wrong materials. If bricks and wood don't pass muster, I'm just not sure they'll go for twigs and leaves."

"Are you trying to wind me up?" Mr Banerjee asked.

"No, sir."

"Without shelter you will quickly succumb to hypothermia. A basic shelter is your priority."

Jagger raised his hand. "Mr Banerjee, sir? What about water? Surely water is a priority?"

Mr Banerjee shook his head. "You can survive three days without water. And in an emergency, there are other solutions. Do you know what I did, during The War?"

(None of us were sure which "war" Mr Banerjee had been in, but from the times he'd mentioned it, it sounded pretty bad. I'm unclear as to the exact dates, but it sounded like it involved hordes of brain-eating zombies, and I guess due to supply shortages all Mr

Banerjee was armed with was a paintball gun.)

"I DRANK MY OWN WEE!" Mr Banerjee announced.

I'd never known year six to be so silent. I think we were all in shock.

"If you're out of water, drink your own wee!" Mr Banerjee repeated.

I muttered to Jagger, "This puts a whole new spin on the lemonade stand Mr Banerjee was running at last year's summer gala."

Jagger dry heaved. "I had four glasses of that stuff!"

Mr Banerjee wasn't done yet. "SCENARIO! While building a survival bunker for a nuclear war, you SEVER A FINGER IN A CIRCULAR SAW! Think fast! What do you do?"

There were assorted suggestions from my classmates, including, "Faint!", "Ask your phone to call an ambulance!" and, probably most sensibly, "Check YouTube for a tutorial," all of which Mr Banerjee rejected, before telling us:

"Pack the stricken finger in ice! A packet of frozen peas is ideal. Putting it on ice will help preserve it until you can get medical attention and have the finger reattached!"

"I wish Miss Percival wasn't getting married," Jagger whispered.

I knew what he meant. This was all pretty stressful for a Friday afternoon.

"Now, year six, I have some exciting news!" Mr Banerjee said.

We all sat up. I hoped the news was that he had cake and we were all having a slice before home time. That, or doughnuts. Or any kind of food, really.

"Since Miss Percival is going on her honeymoon, we have the pleasure of one another's company all next week!"

I looked around at the fixed smiles from all my classmates as we all tried to mask our horror at this development.

"And we're going to do a special themed week!" Mr Banerjee continued, a definite twinkle in his eye. He pointed at the sky out the window. "ASTEROID STRIKE!"

"ARGH!" I screamed, covering my head. I waited

for the impact ... that didn't come. I glanced up. Oh, he didn't mean right now.

"YES!" Mr Banerjee said, rubbing his hands together. "We'll be working on a scenario where an asteroid is due to hit Earth, wiping out life as we know it. In maths, we'll be working out the path of the asteroid; English will see us creating diaries of the aftermath, as we imagine life without electricity, food *or hope*; and music will see us compose our own songs about the asteroid, since there will be no wifi, no screens, no social media, no TV, no anything, and this will be the only form of entertainment." Mr Banerjee grabbed a guitar from behind his desk and strummed a mournful chord.

BiG ROCK FROM OUT-ER SPACE!

Not for the first time, I began to wonder if Mr Banerjee was a little bit off his rocker and maybe that was why he'd had to leave the army and become a teacher instead.

Jagger blew out a breath. "I can't listen to this," he whispered. He put his hand up again.

"Mr Jung?" Mr Banerjee said, pausing his song.

"Where's Miss Percival going on honeymoon?"

Mr Banerjee smiled and put down his guitar. "Sumatra, in Indonesia. Do you know a fact about Sumatra?"

We all shook our heads.

"It's the location of one of the world's super volcanoes!"

Jagger's eyes widened. "What does that mean, sir?"

"It means if that thing blows, you'll never see Miss Percival again." Mr Banerjee shook his head, and muttered, "But that's what you get for booking your honeymoon during term time and expecting your overstretched colleagues to pick up the pieces." He clapped his hands together. "We have forty minutes left, so make a start on your survival bunker designs! I shall sing to inspire you." He struck another chord on his guitar.

The class erupted into a hum of activity as we all got

paper and pens out and started work, trying to ignore Mr Banerjee and his warbling all about our imminent demise.

Jagger drew a large rectangle on his paper as an outline for his survival bunker. He chewed his pen, deep in thought, then scribbled *Gaming room with free Coke machine* inside the rectangle. "Finished!" he said. He glanced at me and smiled. "How's our epic weekend plan looking?"

"*So* epic!" I nodded slowly, to highlight the epicness. "I'm going to ask Mum if we can order pizza *and* barbecue chicken wings, and I reckon she'll agree to ice-cream sundaes as long as..." I glanced at Jagger.

Jagger grinned. "No pranking?"

I nodded.

"I'll be good as gold, promise!"

I already knew that was a lie. At the very least, he would plant a fake dog poo on our sofa, or put itching powder in my boxers.

"Anyway," Jagger continued. "That already sounds like a better weekend than any of this lot will be having."

"Oh, yeah, totally!" I said, glancing around the rest of my class.

"Totally!" Jagger repeated. "Like, not even in the same league!"

"Nowhere near it!"

"Their weekend plans don't come anywhere near the total awesomeness of our weekend plans!"

"As if!" I laughed.

Our plan was just fine.

CHAPTER 2
EVERYONE ELSE'S AWESOME PLAN

If you must know what everyone else's plan was – and I mean, this was so small-fry compared to ours it's barely worth mentioning, so this will be a really short chapter that's so unimportant it might well be cut – it was this:

Rocco Rococo's eleventh birthday party.

Sorry, that font needs to be way less impressive-looking.

ROCCO ROCOCO'S
ELEVENTH BIRTHDAY PARTY.

Better. Now, OK, sure, Rocco had form where his birthday parties were concerned. They were meant to be pretty good. I'd never been invited to one, so I only had school legend to go on, but if that's to be believed, on his eighth birthday, Rocco's parents took him *and his guests* to actual Disney World in America. Flights, hotels, the lot. His ninth birthday was a more subdued affair, with only a trip to see *The Lion King* ... with the best seats in the theatre, a VIP reception in the interval, followed by a backstage tour and a private party where the cast came to sing show tunes while everyone tucked in to Rocco's birthday cake, which had, I kid you not, actual *gold* decorating it. "Happy tenth birthday, Rocco!" shouted *Ariana Grande herself* the following year, at the private concert his parents had arranged. I mean, you get the picture. His birthday parties were ... a bit better than average. And it sounded like his eleventh was going to be the most "a bit better than average" yet. The details were being kept heavily under wraps, but it was rumoured to involve a sleepover, and ever since half term, golden, embossed invites had been appearing on people's desks, or in people's bags, inviting them to this wondrous affair. I mean, I say "wondrous" but I could just as easily say "rather over-the-top, borderline tacky". Money isn't everything and you don't need to spend loads of it to have fun. Point in fact: Jagger and I would have just as much, if not *more* fun over the weekend just by hanging out together and seeing how many Laughing Cow cheese triangles we could fit in our mouths before being sick. We were so excited for that ... which is just as well, since we were the only two people in our class who hadn't been invited to Rocco's.

Do you know how it feels, not to be part of the crowd?

Well, it felt *fine*, because his party would clearly be rubbish anyway.

I wouldn't have gone even if you'd paid me.

Even if you paid me a million pounds.

And on that point, I was very firm.

CHAPTER 3
PLAN B

Jagger chewed his pen again. "I'm gonna add a KFC to my survival bunker," he announced, getting back to work.

I scribbled furiously on my own paper, but it was no good: my pen had run out. "Jagger? Can I borrow a pen?"

"'Course!" he said, not looking up from his work, and nonchalantly handing me one.

I turned the pen over in my fingers. "This is a normal pen, yeah?"

"Uh-huh."

"It's not a prank pen?"

"Nope," he said.

"It's not gonna squirt me with water when I press it or anything?"

"Just a normal pen," Jagger confirmed, busy drawing a little counter in his bunker, complete with a menu board advertising *Free Bargain Buckets*.

I nodded, held the pen at arm's length, and clicked the little button on the top.

And the nib popped out the other end.

Huh. Seemed like I'd done Jagger a disservice. Maybe he wasn't always playing practical jokes for his own amusement. He *could* be trusted. I pressed the nib on to the paper to draw my first—

"AHHHHH!" I screamed, as a FLASH came from the pen and SMOKE started billowing out of it. "Normal pen, you said!"

Jagger was in hysterics. "Yeah! Just a normal pen ... THE EXPLODES WHEN YOU USE IT, HAHAHA!"

I threw the pen down on the table, super-unimpressed. "Oh, yeah. Hilarious. Oh, my splitting sides." No doubt about it, Jagger pushed his luck sometimes. But deep down, I didn't really mind, because we were a team – a couple of otherwise "friendless dorks" (Jack Jones's words – *nice!*) who no one else wanted around them. See, we're both too uncool to be with the cool kids, not sporty enough to be with the sports kids, not talented enough to be with the Drama Darlings, and neither of us can work out the rules of chess, so that cuts out the chess gang. And you know what? *I was fine with that.* We were what we were – Otis and Jagger – two dorks who had each other.

Mr Banerjee remained unaware of all the exploding pen drama, since he was still strumming his guitar, eyes closed, singing a chorus about the merits of stockpiling tins of food.

But someone else *had* noticed. Someone far worse.

The Chloes

I should point out that I said some*one* had noticed, and the Chloes were obviously three people – Posh Chloe, Sporty Chloe and Other Chloe. Well, have you ever seen a science fiction film where you have these evil beings who basically don't think for themselves, but are connected to some sort of hive mind? That's the Chloes. Posh Chloe is the queen, and Sporty Chloe and Other Chloe just echo whatever she says or does. And right at that moment, the Chloes were all staring at me and Jagger in the most terrifying way. Their feelings towards us have always been pretty clear. It's a mixture of pity – like when you see a mangy old mutt in a dog shelter, and you feel kinda sorry for him, but wouldn't actually take him home because he's got fleas, is a bit smelly, and isn't pretty enough – and pure *revulsion*. Like when Mum was clearing out our shed, lifted out an old box, and five rats wriggled out. This reaction to us is what you call an *injustice*, because Jagger and I really aren't so bad, and yet the Chloes would often pass us in the corridor and simply say "Ew!" like we're gross. And, OK, one time I *did* have my hands down my pants, trying to de-wedgie my boxers, and one time Jagger was engaged in a totally legit experiment to see if he could lick out his own belly-button fluff, but those are stand-alone incidents, and not representative of the real us.

The Chloes are Rocco's besties – they're a squad too, just like me and Jagger. They have things called "pamper nights" which seem to involve smearing mud over their faces and putting bits of salad over their eyes, and they all know a lot about fashion and which celebrity is dating who. I feel very inferior compared to them, and I guess, maybe, I am. Bottom line: me and Jagger just aren't cool enough to get invited to Rocco's party – Rocco would never want us there, dorking the place up.

"They're probably staring because they're jealous," Jagger said.

I hooted with laugher. "What are they jealous of?"

"My good looks and your charming personality."

I laughed again, then caught sight of some movement out of the corner of my eye. "Oh, my days!" I gulped. "The Chloes are coming over to us. Act normal! Act normal!"

"We're going to really struggle to do that," Jagger said.

"Well, just act not too weird, then!"

Jagger screwed his face up. "Ah, man, you need

23

to chill out!" He whistled, then glanced up, cool as a cucumber, at the Chloes, who were now looming over our table. "Afternoon, ladies!"

"Good afternoon, Jagger. *Otis*," Posh Chloe said.

"Good afternoon, Jagger. *Otis*," Sporty Chloe and Other Chloe echoed.

The Chloes all had fabulous hair, and all wore matching pinafore dresses, although Posh Chloe had a *Prefect* badge on hers, Sporty Chloe had a *Netball Captain* badge on hers, and Other Chloe ... well, I noticed she just had a button missing. I hoped she wouldn't get in trouble with Posh and Sporty for letting the side down.

"If we'd known you were coming over, we'd have tidied the place up a bit," Jagger said, brushing some pencil sharpenings and bits of rubber off our table. "Won't you sit down?"

"Can I get you a Hobnob?" I asked.

Jagger turned to me. "Have we got Hobnobs?"

"No, I just said it."

"That's a weird thing to say!"

"It's what my mum says when we have guests," I

babbled. "Unless we don't have any Hobnobs. Then maybe she'll ask if they want a custard cream. Or a fig roll."

"Oh, I can't stand them," Jagger said.

"That's fascinating, boys," Posh Chloe said. "But I'm not here for your scintillating biscuit chat."

"Ooh! 'Scintillating!'" Jagger grinned. "Someone's been hanging around the vocabulary display again!" He gestured towards the display that Miss Percival had put up on the wall, featuring words it would be good to use in our written work. One of the words was *miniscule*. Another was *posterior*. I felt like the display was trolling me.

"Just try to keep up, Jagger," Posh Chloe said, looking with disgust at the small stain on his sweatshirt. "What *is* that?"

"Mayonnaise from the chicken wrap served at lunch," Jagger replied, without missing a beat. It wasn't. It was from where he'd accidentally snotted on himself during break. Another stand-alone incident, definitely not representative of the real us.

"I'll cut to the chase," Posh Chloe said, "since none

of us need this horrific conversation to last any longer than necessary."

I blinked at her. She was very good at words.

"I come bearing a missive," she said.

Jagger squinted at her. "A what?"

"A missive," she repeated. She must have clocked our confused faces, because she then added, "An important letter! Actually, an *invitation*."

And with that she dropped two golden envelopes on our table.

I stared down at my envelope. It had a coat of arms on the front, bearing the motto:

Rocco est splendidus

"What does that mean?" I asked.

"Rocco is glorious," Posh Chloe replied. "It's Latin."

"Latin…" I repeated, tracing my fingers over the embossing, and then over my name, which was written in the middle of the envelope in a very fancy way. A golden envelope. With Rocco's coat of arms. It could only mean…

I glanced over to where Rocco was sitting, but he was busy with his work, using his posh propelling pencil and the set square from his fancy maths set to design his bunker. I'd never even spoken to Rocco. I wasn't sure he even knew I existed, or, if he did, he doubtless saw himself as so important and perfect, and me as so unimportant and imperfect, that he'd never bother to acknowledge me.

The faintest hint of a smile flickered at the corners of Posh Chloe's mouth. "Why don't you open it?"

I glanced at Jagger, whose eyes were as wide as mine felt. Was this really happening? Was it really an invite to the party of the decade? I mean, not that I cared about that and – anyway, hang on, this could actually just be a really mean trick. The Chloes don't like us. What if this was just something to amuse them? Taunting us, by making us think we'd been invited to the party, only for the envelope to be empty, or something. Ha! Well, joke's on them, because we didn't want to go anyway!

Jagger clearly didn't share my fears, though: he ripped open the seal and pulled out the card inside, gasped when he read it, then held it in his hand, frozen, just staring at it. I shook myself into action and ripped mine open too.

Rocco est splendidus

Rocco Rococo Esquire cordially requests the pleasure of your company at the magical celebration of the eleventh year of his birth. A royal feast is to be held, with entertainment to keep you amused. The ball begins on the sixth strike of the town clock, Saturday 5th June. Carriages at 10 p.m. or stay for the sleepover.

I blinked and tried to make sense of the words, which were swimming in front of my eyes. I read it over and over. Was this real? I looked back up at the Chloes, who were smiling back at me – slightly evilly, if I'm honest, but smiling nevertheless.

"Well?" Posh Chloe said, arching one of her manicured eyebrows.

I swallowed. "Rocco? Esquire? Cordially? Royal

feast? Sleepover? Ball?" I babbled.

Posh Chloe rolled her eyes. "Well, that made no sense. Can you come or not?"

"I dunno, we're pretty busy," I managed to say.

"Mmm," Posh Chloe replied, sweeping back her perfect, long blonde hair. "You're so *not* though, are you?" She turned her attention to Jagger. "What about you?"

Jagger chewed his lip, clearly deep in thought. And I knew what he was thinking about. We already had plans. We had our whole weekend mapped out, and it was going to be *great*. We weren't going to drop everything just because this invite from Rocco had—

"We'll be there, we're totally free, we can't wait, we're *so, so, so* excited about this! WOO-HOO!" Jagger screamed.

Huh. So I guessed that was that.

"Great!" Posh Chloe chirped. "Bring sleeping bags and pillows if you want to sleep over – but no synthetic fibres, Rocco is allergic to polyester. Birthday gifts are welcome. Nothing under the value of forty pounds, please." She gave two quick thumps to her chest with her fist. *"Rocco est splendidus!"*

We both stared at her, then realized we were meant to copy. *"Rocco est splendidus!"* we both chorused, thumping our fists on our chests too.

I glanced back at Rocco again, but he didn't seem to have clocked any of this – he was still getting on with his work, composed, silent, his face giving nothing away, his hair so perfectly styled, like it was every day, like he'd just walked out of the barber's. He didn't seem real. Just like this invite.

The Chloes turned and glided away.

"Hasta la vista!" Jagger shouted after them.

"We're doing it, then?" I asked Jagger. "We're gonna go? What about our plan?"

"It's still our plan," Jagger replied. "It's just our Plan B." He lowered his voice a bit. "I heard there's going to be a chocolate fountain!"

"Jagger, we can melt some chocolate ourselves and dip stuff in it!"

"Apparently it's the size of a small swimming pool, as tall as two fully-grown adults, and holds a hundred gallons of molten chocolate."

"Huh," I said.

"I know how you like chocolate."

"I know how *you* like chocolate," I replied.

"So why miss this unique opportunity?"

Jagger did have a point. Chocolate fountains like that aren't the sort of thing you encounter every day – maybe even only once in your lifetime. And while I didn't have any desire to spend time with the Chloes, or the Drama Darlings, or the Football Fanatics, or everyone else who somehow managed to be more cool and a whole lot less dorky than either of us, if Jagger was with me, we'd have a good time anyway. Plus, we could always do our existing weekend plans the following week.

So that's how I reached the decision to say nothing and go along with it.

Big mistake.

CHAPTER 4
BIZARRE SILVER PEACOCK

I hadn't actually been to anyone's birthday party before, other than Jagger's laser tag extravaganzas for just the two of us, and I wasn't entirely sure what the dress code was. I stood in front of the full-length mirror in my mum's room, trying to work out if my latest attempt at an outfit would be acceptable enough. Rocco was always dressed in the best gear, and I had no doubt all his mates would be too.

Unfortunately, due to my mother bulk-buying what I'm pretty sure is counterfeit Disney-themed underwear from a dodgy market trader, I was doomed to wear (for the next thousand years, probably) Mickey Mouse boxers and *Toy Story* socks – one of which already had a hole in the toe due to the shoddy fabric. That's fine, because no one would be seeing my boxers or socks anyway, but I would have preferred the confidence boost that *quality* underwear apparently gives you (according to Mum's *Modern Woman* magazine). Anyway, my outfit ended up being jeans and trainers, and a smart T-shirt: simple, but classic. Understated, but cool. A sure-fire hit.

"Oh, no, no, no!" I heard Jagger's voice behind me. Mum must have let him in downstairs. I turned, and my mouth dropped open when I saw what *he* had on: silver shorts, silver trainers with silver ankle socks, a silver-sequinned crop top, and huge silver feathers coming up from behind his shoulders. "You can't go like that!" he told me.

"Like *what*?" I spluttered. "What are *you* going as?"

"This is my party outfit," he explained.

"Right," I said. "And the feathers?"

"My *plume*," he corrected me. "You've got to make an impact, Otis! I'm not being rude, but look at yourself. You look ... very average."

"I am average!" I snapped.

Jagger put a finger to my lips to silence me. "Shh, now! Less of that talk, Otis Bumble. Tonight, Jagger and Otis show the world that they are..." He gasped, staring into the middle distance.

"Idiots?" I suggested.

Jagger ignored me. "*Extraordinary!*"

"OK, well, you look like a bizarre peacock that's been spray-painted silver."

"And you look like you're heading out to soft play with your family. Come on, sweet cheeks, we'll spruce you up in no time!"

"Gah!" I groaned, as Jagger shepherded me back through to my bedroom, and started pulling all my clothes out of my wardrobe, holding various outfits up to me, then tutting and throwing them down again.

Twenty minutes later and Jagger had agreed that I could keep my jeans, but only on condition I wear my special disco shirt – which is black and has orange flames around the bottom. The shirt originally belonged to my dad when he was my age. It was something he'd kindly handed down to me ... along with a genetic predisposition for shortness. I'd previously discounted the shirt because I didn't want to be too flashy, and potentially outshine Rocco, but Jagger assured me the shirt was perfect, and I mean, Jagger was already going to outshine *the sun* with his outfit. However, apparently it wasn't quite enough. "You know what would really complete the look? Make-up!" he said.

"I'm good, thanks."

He shook his head. "No arguments. People won't even notice; it'll just enhance your appearance. Can you even tell I'm wearing eyeshadow?"

"The silver glitter? Yes, I can."

"Really? Well, OK. But with you, we'll go more subtle."

After Jagger had pleaded with my mum for access to her make-up bag, he sat me down on my bed, pulled a chair up opposite, and started work on my face.

"I've been thinking," I said, as Jagger gently dabbed around my eyes with a make-up brush. "Well, *worrying*, really. What if this is all a trick, you know? What if, when we get there, they tie us up, then parade us around on leads like performing monkeys, while the real guests laugh and poke us with sticks?"

"Mm, this shade of purple really suits you."

"Jagger? Are you not worried? Don't you think this whole thing is a bit weird? The sudden, last-minute invite? And the look in Posh Chloe's eyes when she came over to us yesterday. She looked … *evil*."

"She always looks evil. She's posh. It's just how posh people look – they can't help it, it's because they're always working out how to get more money." Jagger dabbed another brush in the eyeshadow case. "Now for some green."

"I dunno, I just have a bad feeling," I muttered.

Jagger sighed and sat back a bit. "*Otis*. I think you're wrong, but even if you're right, we're together, so what's the worst that could happen? Me and you against the world, remember? Always have been, always will. No matter what happens."

There was something weird in the tone of Jagger's voice that I couldn't quite place. "What do you mean, 'no matter what happens'?"

Jagger swallowed, then his face changed back to his usual bubbly and bright expression. "Nothing! It's just a saying, Otis. And what I'm *saying* is, so what if they try to lead us around like performing monkeys—"

"And poke us with sticks!"

"—We'll be fine, because we'll stick together and get ourselves out of it." He smiled at me. "All done! Let's get a quick pic!" He whipped out his phone, scooted around next to me, and took a photo before I could object.

Jagger clearly stuck to his promise that my make-up would be "more subtle" ... *NOT!*

Jagger and I had ~~both sold a kidney~~ clubbed together for Rocco's gift, and Jagger now presented – with a flourish – this Lego Technic mechanical digger thing, with loads of gears and pistons. It looked pretty impressive. "But will *Rocco* be impressed?" I asked, very aware of how grown-up and sophisticated he and the Chloes always were.

"I love that you care about that."

"I just don't want us to look foolish, that's all!" I said, adjusting one of Jagger's feathers that had fallen to the side a bit.

"Otis, it's for twelve-plus years! Rocco's only eleven. This is big-boy Lego, 'course he'll be impressed!"

"Huh," I said. I turned the box over to look at the back and then spotted the price tag. "£39.99?! Posh Chloe said all gifts had to have a minimum value of £40! This is a disaster!"

"One step ahead of you!" Jagger grinned and pulled a shiny penny out of the pocket of his silver shorts. "We'll just Sellotape this to the box, and *voila!* It now has a value of exactly forty pounds!"

"Genius! I'll write a gift tag, you do the wrapping," I said.

I set to work, writing Rocco's name on the tag. Quite why, if your surname was *Rococo*, you would call your child *Rocco*, I had no idea. It was a nightmare trying to write his name on that tag: it's mainly just *O*s and *C*s in various combinations. I made so many mistakes, I started running out of tags, and he ended up with one that had a reindeer on the front and said *Merry Christmas!* inside.

Gift wrapped and (eventually) tagged, Jagger sprayed

us both with something called "Old Spice", which he'd borrowed from his dad. "You smell *divine!*" he told me.

I wasn't entirely sure. "Do I?"

Jagger nodded. "Trust me. People often tell Dad it smells 'pungent'. That's another word for strong. So now we're powerful, right?"

"I guess." I wasn't sure why being powerful was necessary for the party.

Suited and booted, we trotted downstairs where my mum told us we both looked very "memorable".

"You're sure you don't mind us going?" I said to Mum.

"Otis, I'm devastated you both won't be here to keep me company tonight – I'll be so, so lonely just having a quiet bath by myself with some candles and essential oils – but I think it'll be nice for you two to make friends with everyone else in your class."

"Why would we want to do that?" I put my arm across Jagger's shoulders and pulled him close. "No one's better than Jagger!"

Jagger laughed. "And no one's better than you, my friend!"

I grinned.

"But," he continued, "at the same time, it does no harm to hang out with new people, maybe … make more friends!"

My eyes widened. Never, in our whole six years of friendship, had the need for extra friends ever been mentioned. *"What's going on?"*

Jagger blinked back at me. "Nothing's going on! Let's just have an awesome night!"

I stared at him.

"You'll have a lovely time!" Mum said. "Come here!" She gave me a hug and then started choking. "Gosh, you certainly smell … *pungent!*"

I glanced at Jagger, who gave me a thumbs up.

"Now, let's do a final check," Mum said, extracting herself from me and grabbing a clipboard from the table. Mum's a traffic warden – a job she loves, because she's a stickler for rules. When she found out this wasn't just a party, but an actual sleepover, she went into manic planning mode, making sure I had everything I needed, and double-checking what everyone else was taking on the parents' WhatsApp group chat. "Sleeping bag?" she said.

"Check!" I replied.

"Wash bag with toothpaste, toothbrush, shower gel and the special cream for your sore—"

"CHECK!" I shouted, before she could finish *that* sentence.

"Pants."

"Check."

"Spare pants?"

"I don't need spare pants, I'm not three!"

Mum pursed her lips. "Suppose Rocco has a pond and you fall in it?"

I locked eyes with her and breathed heavily.

"You know how clumsy you can be, Otis. You'd want to walk around with wet and clammy pants, would you?"

"OK, I'll get some spare pants."

"Spare trousers too, in that case!" Jagger piped up. "And socks! And a top, maybe!"

"Yeah, thanks, I'll just grab a total new outfit *in case I fall in a pond which Rocco may not even have!*"

After I'd got my "pond accident outfit" ready, and

after we'd double-checked everything, and after Mum gave me my usual reminder about not eating too much sugar because of the time I downed five (large) bags of Starmix then tore my shirt off like the Incredible Hulk and ran into a ball pit screaming "GIVE ME ALL THE BALLS!" (I mean, that was years ago – *c'mon, Mum!* ... OK, it was last year, but that's still ages), we crammed ourselves in the back of our tiny Nissan Micra and set off for Rocco's house, while listening to Mum complain about various parking violations she spotted along the way. "On a double yellow, that would be an instant ticket!" she exclaimed, seeing one parked car as we passed by. "The sign clearly says no parking on the weekend, so that's a tow-away in my book!" she said of another.

Pretty soon the streets became noticeably more leafy, and the houses noticeably bigger. Our town isn't huge, but I'd only been to this part of it once – me and Jagger rode our bikes round here about a year ago, and after enduring several people spying on us from behind their curtains, a man who shouted at us for accidentally riding on a bit of his lawn, and a woman who claimed to have called the police because "we looked like trouble", we'd never been back.

"Right boys, we're almost there," Mum said. "But Rocco's house is on a road with residents-only parking, so I'm not sure where I'll be able to stop."

"Mum, really?" I said. "Couldn't you just pull over, like, for a second?"

Mum laughed. "Good god, Otis! Why don't you just ask me to commit a murder while you're at it?! No. Stopping is forbidden, so we'll need to find a *legal* parking area."

Half an hour later, and Mum had found a legal parking area ... just around the corner from where we'd started, at our house. "You can just walk the rest of the way," Mum muttered.

"But we've got luggage, and it's at least an hour away!" I pleaded.

"I could walk it in ten minutes," Mum replied.

"But it'll take us longer – we've got shorter legs!"

"Well, one day you'll grow, Otis. There will be other changes too, for example—"

"NOT NOW, MUM!" I snapped, scrambling out

43

of the car and heaving my wheelie case after me. She knows the threat of mentioning anything that was covered in our "Healthy Bodies" class makes me shift faster than lightning. It's an unfair move.

Jagger and I started striding along the pavement, pulling our cases behind us. We were going to arrive late now.

"Walk faster!" I told Jagger.

"I can't, my feathers are providing wind resistance!"

At that point, my mum, worried about potential kidnappers (despite once telling me that any kidnapper would "hand me back within minutes because I'm so desperately annoying"), sailed past in our car as she tracked us, shouting through the open window, "Have a good night and try not to be too weird!"

"Cheers, Mum!" I said, giving her the thumbs up as she disappeared again down the road. *Try not to be too weird*? I mean, (a) had she seen what the pair of us looked like? And (b) like she's the expert in not being "weird" anyway!

Five minutes later, we were both *shattered* – like, practically dead, to be honest – the wind was really getting up, and Jagger was in grave danger of being lifted into the air thanks to his *plume*.

"I'm beginning to wish I'd tried harder in PE," I gasped.

"I am sweating in places I don't normally sweat," Jagger replied.

"Don't have too much sugar, Otis!" Mum shouted out of the open car window, as she sailed past again. "You know you get silly if you have too much sugar!"

"Yep, thanks, Mum!" I shouted back.

She disappeared out of sight.

And then it started raining.

Ten minutes later, we looked up, wet, sweaty and bedraggled, but totally awestruck, at the massive house that was sitting at the end of the wide, gravelled driveway. A plaque on the wall read *Rococo Residence*. "Guess this is it, then!" I said, flapping my sticky shirt about to cool me down. I took a deep breath, and as Jagger and I crunched up the driveway, I swear the rain clouds parted, the wind calmed to a gentle breeze, and the sun came out. Rich people never have bad weather, it seems.

We approached the huge wooden front door, pulled a little chain to the left, and waited as a peal of bells sounded from inside.

"I still feel nervous," I said.

"Don't be," Jagger replied. "We're gonna have an amazing night."

"Maybe," I muttered.

I don't know, I just couldn't shake the feeling something bad was going to happen. This wasn't helped when a tall girl with glossy dark brown hair, enormous eyebrows, and even more enormous eyelashes answered the door, and glanced us up and down with disdain. "It isn't fancy dress," she said.

"And we're not *in* fancy dress!" Jagger replied.

"OK, whatever." The girl checked our names against the guest list, just as Mum sailed past the end of the driveway again, leaning out of the car window and shouting at us.

"If he starts itching his—"

"MUM!" I squealed.

"He's got some special cream which he just needs to gently apply up his—"

"THANKS, MUM, BYE!"

The tall girl glanced down at me and curled her purple, glossy lip. "OK, *gross*," she said.

And with that, she stepped aside, ushered us both in and closed the heavy door firmly behind us.

CHAPTER 5
TAYLOR SWIFT

The tall girl led us in silence through a long hallway, which had various doors off to either side. The cream carpet was so soft it was like walking through fresh snow. This was a truly amazing house – but it was no house for a party. For a start, there were huge vases with intricate designs displayed on plinths as we walked along. I don't know much about vases, but I do know they're the sorts of things that are often highly valuable, and get broken VERY easily. Especially at parties. So that seemed weird. Meanwhile, on the walls, they had all these massive old paintings. They weren't to my taste – I don't know why you'd want pictures of some old sunflowers, or a girl with pearl earrings, or a woman who has a weird half smile on her face – but they also looked like they might have cost at least fifty pounds, if not seventy, so, again, you don't need to be Einstein to know they shouldn't be on display at a kid's birthday party.

The eerie silence, the precious vases, the expensive paintings, the luxury cream carpet – all of this made me more nervous that this was all some kind of trick and this tall girl was actually leading us straight into the room where WE WOULD BE PARADED AROUND LIKE PERFORMING MONKEYS AND POKED WITH STICKS!

"So, are you friends with Rocco?" the girl eventually asked.

"YEP!" we both lied.

"OK, then you're not the weirdo boys that Rocco added yesterday at the last minute."

Jagger and I glanced at each other.

"Nope!" Jagger said. "No idea who *those* boys would be. We're" – he blew out a breath – "practically his besties."

I nodded. "Such good mates."

"Best buds!"

"Friends till the end!"

"Super pals, total chums, complete bros!"

"Please don't poke us with sticks!"

Jagger jabbed me in the side to shut me up. "And how about you?" Jagger asked the girl.

"I'm Coco, his older sister," the girl replied, not looking at us.

"*Coco Rococo?!*" Jagger mouthed at me.

"It's difficult being a model, influencer and activist," she continued, "when your work is always being interrupted by pre-teen boys and their *friends.*" She turned and glared at us, then sniffed. "And what *is* that smell?"

"*That*," I said, confidently, "is Stale Spices."

"*Old* Spices!" Jagger hissed.

"It's *pungent*," Coco said.

I grinned. "Thanks!" Jagger was right. This fragrance was a *hit*. Everyone loved it. We were set to be the talk (and smell!) of the party.

We carried on following Coco as she led us through a huge kitchen that had ten ovens, then out through some huge sliding glass doors and into the garden.

We both gasped as we looked out in front of us.

The garden (which was HUGE, by the way, seriously, most parks aren't even this big) had a massive marquee in the centre of it, with gold and silver balloons forming an arch around the glitter-curtained entrance and the beat of music coming from inside. Outside, on the lawn by the entrance, were fire jugglers, stilt walkers and unicyclists, all entertaining the stream of Rocco's friends who were heading inside the marquee. Beyond the marquee – *was I dreaming?* – was some sort of ACTUAL FAIRGROUND! There was a big wheel, dodgems, some waltzers, a ghost train and something very big, high and scary called "The Terminator", which looked like it shot its riders up to the top of a huge tower and then dropped them back down again.

I looked at Jagger, who had his mouth hanging open. This wasn't just a birthday party. This was the Eighth Wonder of the World!

"There's a cloakroom for your sleepover stuff just inside the entrance," Coco said, looking utterly bored, and like she saw this sort of thing every day. "Bye." She turned and went back inside the house.

"*Weirdo boys!*" I said to Jagger. "That's what Coco said! She means us!"

"We don't know that!"

"Who else only got their invites yesterday?"

Jagger shrugged. "We only know about our class, though. Rocco will have other friends. From other schools. Maybe even from abroad. He's glamorous like that."

I sighed. I was still worried: apart from anything else, why would he even invite us if he thinks we're weird? But the party *did* look incredible. "Come on, then," I said. "Let's go and find Rocco and give him his present."

Outside the marquee was awesome enough, but inside was ... I don't know. I don't know what's better than awesome? Super awesome? Mega awesome?

Awesome to the power of ten billion? OK, so it was quite dark inside, but coloured lights illuminated the roof and walls, including moving spotlights that shone bright beams across the space, and glitter balls that made everything look like it was swimming in diamonds. At the far end of the marquee was a stage – like something you'd see at a rock concert, with a huge lighting rig and massive speakers. In front of that was an area for an audience, with lots of little tables for people to sit around. And in front of that, closest to us, was a big dance floor, with a DJ booth and a dry-ice machine that was pumping out this magical, billowing mist all over the floor, where Kyle, Layla and Florence (AKA the Drama Darlings) were already shaking their groove thing to a song about it "raining men". Meanwhile, around the edge of the tent were loads of food carts. Whatever you wanted to eat, it was there, and it was free: tacos, crêpes, burgers, hot dogs, barbecued chicken wings, crispy duck pancakes, fresh popcorn, candy floss, and the giant chocolate fountain (which was *ma-hoo*-sive, just like Jagger had said) where Jake, Jack and Jon (the football lads) were squealing with delight, dipping everything from strawberries and banana to pretzels and marshmallows in the cascades of molten chocolate. There was even a vast pick 'n' mix stand with every sort of sweet you've ever seen, which the twins Mimi and Matty (our class's "account monitored by Mum" YouTubers) were busy filming and simultaneously munching their way through. Then there were drinks counters serving everything from Slush to fresh smoothies, and a *mock*tails stand, where a bartender would pour the concoction of your choice through an ice sculpture of a unicorn doing a handstand, with the perfectly chilled drink coming out of its upside-down horn, straight into your glass.

This was the stuff of DREAMS!

In an adjoining marquee to the left, they'd set up a ten-pin bowling alley, laser quest, an arcade with loads of video games, VR simulators, and a massive ball pit, currently occupied by a load of kids I'd never seen before, who must be other mates of Rocco's. In another tent to the right, there was a chill-out area full of huge beanbags, cushions and a booth serving milkshakes you could have any chocolate bar blended into. Some of the year six chess club were having the time of their lives playing a game on the giant chess set, with bishops, rooks and pawns as tall as they were.

"Wow!" Jagger said, taking it all in.

"Wow!" I agreed.

"Wow," a random kid said as he passed by, looking me and Jagger up and down. It was true: we were in the wrong gear. Everyone else was dressed in casual stuff – jeans, T-shirts, just normal. Only "the weirdo" boys had come dressed … weird. But it was fairly dark, so maybe most people wouldn't notice?

After we'd stood and stared at everything in disbelief for about five minutes, we ventured further inside, looking for Rocco. But there was too much to see, do, eat and drink, so it went something like:

"Come on, maybe he's over… Ooh! Fresh doughnuts!" And then Jagger and I would cram our faces with doughnuts for three minutes. And then I'd say, "OK, now we really must find him, maybe we should try… Ooh! A magician!" And one of the walkabout entertainers would perform a card trick in front of us, which culminated in me finding the chosen card *in my actual shoe!* And then Jagger discovered a food cart serving little boxes of fish and chips, I downed a small bowl of pad thai, we feasted on churros and dipped them in the chocolate fountain, ate some ice cream, and finished up with a couple of bao buns, which turned out to be a most delicious type of Chinese food.

"We really must stop eating," I said, eating five arancini balls in quick succession.

"Would you like some Turkish baklava?" Jagger asked.

"Yes, please," I mumbled, my mouth already full of some falafel I'd just picked up.

It was then I spotted something I hadn't seen before. A curtained-off area, towards the back of the main marquee, with a red rope hanging across the entrance. I nudged Jagger. "What's in there, do you reckon?"

"Probably something even more amazing than all these amazing things so far," Jagger said. "It must be the VIP area."

I gave him a quizzical look.

"VIP! 'Very Important Person!' And we definitely have to go and check it out."

We walked up to the red rope, looked around to see if anyone was going to stop us, then jumped over it, heading around one of the big billowing drapes, and there he was ... Rocco Rococo.

His dark hair was as perfectly styled as always; his handsome face composed, as if nothing about any of this party held in his honour impressed or excited him. The suit he wore was doubtless expertly tailored, but without a tie, and with open-necked shirt, he didn't look too formal, just *sophisticated* and *cool*. Light glinted off his bright, white teeth, which had turned out completely straight and would never need a brace. Everything about this magical boy gave off the aura of perfection and wealth ... even before we get to the fact he was sitting on an actual golden THRONE surrounded by the Chloes and piles of his birthday presents, while TAYLOR SWIFT fed him peeled grapes from a silver platter.

I had no idea what was going on. Rocco looked up from unwrapping a big box that was sitting on his lap. "Ah," he smiled, putting the gift aside. "Otis and Jagger. *I've been expecting you.*"

I'm not sure if he was deliberately trying to sound like a James Bond villain, but honestly, if he'd then done an evil laugh while stroking a white cat, and then tied us both down to a conveyor belt heading towards a laser beam, I would not have been surprised.

"*Rocco est splendidus!*" Jagger said, thumping his chest.

"*Rocco est spendidus!*" I mumbled.

Rocco raised an eyebrow, looked slightly amused by this, then turned to Taylor Swift and said, "No more grapes, thank you." Taylor nodded and scuttled away through an exit behind the throne.

I pointed in her direction. "Was that...?"

"Lookalike," Rocco explained.

"Oh!" I said. "Of course."

"I'm actually just having a quiet birthday lunch with the real Taylor Swift when I see her in LA over the summer."

I nodded. I couldn't tell if he was serious or not. Based on this party, I was edging towards him being serious.

"Brave choice of shirt," Rocco told me.

"Thanks?"

"And you" – he lazily gestured towards Jagger from his throne – "is that a Vivienne Westwood?"

Jagger turned to me, and I shrugged. "Yeeeees?" Jagger hedged his bets.

Rocco nodded, thoughtfully.

I glanced at all the gifts he was surrounded by – a laptop, two tablets, headphones, an electric guitar, several really impressive-looking drones, and various large bags that had words like *Chanel* and *Harrods* written on them. I gulped. Compared to all this stuff, our Lego seemed ... babyish. Would Rocco think we were babyish too? That the Chloes were right about us?

"We got you a present!" I said, as brightly as I could. Jagger handed it over.

Rocco smiled, and looked at the name tag. "Wow. You actually spelled my name right."

I nodded. "Of course! Tenth time lucky, haha!"

"Merry Christmas?" He frowned, reading the print inside the tag.

"Good to get it in early! Hahahahaha!" I replied.

Rocco didn't laugh back, but set about carefully peeling away the wrapping paper, while the Chloes looked on. I'd never seen anyone open a present so slowly and carefully. With the paper all removed, he lifted the Lego box up, turning it over in his hands, examining it, his face giving nothing away. Then he looked up. "Thank you." He stared at me for a few moments. "I love it," he added, flatly.

I could feel my pulse increasing. Even though he was in my class, this was the most I'd ever spoken to Rocco. He made me feel … unworthy, somehow. I didn't like it. Ugh. Who was I kidding? However much my mum might have wanted me to, I didn't fit in here, and there was no point in trying. That's why Jagger and me were best mates. We just *fit*. Neither of us had to try.

"What other presents did you get?" Jagger asked.

Posh Chloe stepped forwards. "Gold!"

"Frankincense!" Sporty Chloe added.

Other Chloe swallowed. "And … a giant Toblerone. I didn't get the memo about the 'gold, frankincense' thing." She looked down sheepishly. She already looked a bit out of place, wearing that weird headdress with the bendy springs with pom-poms on the end; I wondered whether Posh and Sporty Chloe had approved this, or whether she had gone rogue, since their outfits were otherwise identical.

"You may go now," Posh Chloe told us.

"Can I go too?" Other Chloe said, suddenly perking

up. "I'm dying to go in the ball pit and throw some shapes on the dance floor!"

"No!" Posh Chloe hissed. "The ball pit's for kids, and the only thing we're going to be throwing is glances of pity at the non-VIP guests. You must stay here."

"But this isn't fun!" Other Chloe complained.

"It's not about *fun*," Posh Chloe told her. "It's about being *exclusive*."

Other Chloe bowed her head and I started backing out of the VIP area. "Thank you for inviting us," I said.

Rocco's eyes met mine. "Oh, I didn't," he said, just as the curtain closed again in front of us.

CHAPTER 6
FOUNTAIN OF CHOCOLATE GOODNESS

Jagger told me I shouldn't worry about Rocco saying he didn't actually invite us, and that we should just enjoy the incredible party, because what did it matter?

"But if Rocco didn't invite us, then who did … *and why?*" I asked.

Jagger shrugged. "You're overthinking this."

"This is why I prefer it when it's just you and me hanging out. I don't have to worry about things like this," I said. I glanced across the tent to where year six's top sportsperson was demonstrating her skills by bowling strike after strike at the ten-pin bowling alley, to the increasing hysteria of an adoring crowd of my classmates. Nicknamed The G.O.A.T., (as in, Greatest Of All Time, on account of her winning *everything* on the sports field), her actual name was Tiana Abimbola, and she was tall, and strong, and not just outstanding at sport, but brilliant at work stuff too. She made me feel as bad about myself as Rocco did. She was so … capable. And I was so … mediocre?

"I like it best when it's just me and you," I confirmed. Jagger and I could be mediocre together.

"Uh-huh." Jagger swallowed. "But, um … maybe it's good for you to meet other people who could be as good friends as I am."

"But I don't need to."

"But some of our classmates are probably OK people."

"Hang on," I said. "Why did you say it would be good for *me* to meet some new friends, but not *you* as well?"

For a moment, Jagger looked like a startled deer in the headlights of an oncoming car. He opened his mouth. Then closed it again.

"Jagger?" I said.

"I was going to tell you. I was going to tell you this weekend, at yours, but then this party came up, and I figured if tonight went well, it would kind of help things, and we'd both feel better about it because you wouldn't be alone so it wouldn't matter!"

I crossed my arms. "What are you talking about?"

"I got in to the Barbara Scarborough School of Performing Arts!" Jagger blurted out. "They wrote to my mum last week. They've offered me a scholarship. I totally didn't want to go, but they've got a track record of creating child stars, and that ticked a lot of boxes for my mum. She says I have to take the opportunity and that most kids would kill for a free place. So ... I start there in September. Which means..." He trailed off, and looked down at the floor while the full horror of what he was saying slammed into me like a double-decker bus.

"Which means you won't be at Grimstone High with me?"

Jagger nodded. "I'll still be in town – we can totally

see each other at weekends, and holidays, and even after school, but…"

"I'll be on my own. In a new school. With seriously big kids, some of whom have facial hair, and you won't be with me, and I'll have no one, and that's why you wanted me to make some new friends because otherwise I AM GONNA BE BEATEN TO A PULP IN THE CORRIDORS BECAUSE THEY ALWAYS PICK OFF THE WEAKEST FIRST – OH, JAGGER!"

I'm not embarrassed to admit it, I started crying.

"Calm down, Otis! It'll be fine!" Jagger bare-faced lied to me. "Once you get to know the rest of our class better, you'll have loads of options for more friends." He scanned the marquee. "What about Jake, Jack and Jon?"

"The football lads?!" I howled. "I don't know about … goals … and stuff! We've nothing in common!"

"Kyle, then? Or one of the Drama Darlings? You're being quite dramatic now, Otis!"

I sniffed back tears. "It's you I want!" I stumbled over to the pick 'n' mix stand. "I'm not being rude," I mumbled, cramming my mouth with comforting cola bottles, foam bananas and some Haribo fried eggs, "but

I heard your audition song. Are you sure they haven't made a mistake? You applied as a joke, after all!"

Jagger nodded. "Yeah, no, that's what I thought too, but they said it was 'bold and daring'."

"Oh. Then I suppose it must be good," I said, sadly. I suddenly felt bad. I should be pleased for Jagger's achievements, rather than only thinking of myself. "I'm sorry. I just don't want to lose you," I muttered.

Jagger picked up a foam shrimp, chucked it in the air and caught it in his mouth. "It'll be all right, Otis. You'll see."

"Jagger?" I said, quietly. "Well done. I know it's hard to get into that school. You did well."

His eyes met mine and he smiled. "Thanks, Otis. Now, let's remember I'm not gone yet, so let's have a nice night. And maybe we'll find you a new friend or two along the way, OK?"

"OK," I said.

Jagger dragged me around the marquee, doing his best to take my mind off things, but everything just seemed to remind me I was going to lose him. He interrogated the sword swallower about whether his act was a trick or real (apparently, it's real, it's just a case of clearing your mind, staying calm and "relaxing" various muscles in your throat to enable the sword to go down – I mean, *really*? That still seems super dangerous to me, and also *why would you?*), but it just reminded me of all the tricks and pranks Jagger plays, and how much they make me laugh, and how much I'll miss having that at Grimstone High.

Then we did laser quest, and Jagger shouted, "I'll cover you!" and as I stormed across an open patch of space on the course, I thought to myself, *But you won't be able to "cover me" at Grimstone High, BECAUSE YOU WON'T BE THERE!*

When we got back into the main marquee, a magician had Sporty Chloe in a box on stage, and was in the process of chopping her in half. Everyone gasped as Sporty Chloe was split in two. I looked, miserably, towards the stage. That's how I felt! Like I'd already lost my other half. I was going to be Bert without my Ernie, Spongebob without my Patrick, mac without my cheese.

Jagger turned to me, as we watched the two halves

of Chloe be put back together from the back. "Thank goodness the trick didn't go wrong."

"Yes." I smirked, in spite of myself. "That would have been truly terrible."

Jagger tapped my chest with the back of his hand. "Maybe that's how the Chloes replicate? You know, they sort of divide themselves?"

"Like ... aliens?"

"I think they're here to supplant the human race," he said.

We both laughed again.

"What's funny, boys?" I whipped round to find Posh Chloe right behind me, looking really unamused.

"N-nothing!" I said.

She stepped towards me and whispered in my ear. "We see and hear *everything*."

I froze as a shiver ran through me. In the unlikely, yet still possible, event the Chloes really were aliens, they now knew that Jagger and I knew their secret! Were we in danger?

Posh Chloe stepped back again, lurking just a metre or so behind me and Jagger, like a fart that no one wanted to admit to and you wished would just go away. We tried to focus our attention back on the stage.

The next act introduced himself as Enzo the Enchanter, a stage hypnotist. He was a tall, wiry man, with a funny little bit of beard on the end of his long chin, a top hat, and a cloak covered in stars. After a lot of Enzo sweeping his hands around and telling us how mystical he was, he invited Rocco up on to the stage, to loud cheers and whoops from the crowd. Rocco did a bow, clearly loving every second of being the big, important birthday boy, and went to take his seat on the end of a row of four chairs.

"Now!" Enzo boomed. "How about, for a bit of fun, we also get your family up here too, Rocco? Hmm?"

The crowd laughed – that did sound pretty cool.

"Um … they're not actually here," Rocco said. "They're having a quiet night inside the house, watching a movie." He glanced down at the floor, and, for a moment, he almost looked a bit sad.

"But ... it's your birthday!" Enzo said, looking confused.

"Yeah, but ... only my eleventh," Rocco replied. "Like Dad says, it's not like it's an important one." He swallowed. "But, hey!" he continued, suddenly perking up. "Who wants dorky parents and older sisters around anyway?"

Everyone laughed again ... everyone except Enzo, who was frowning at Rocco, and rubbing his chin with his fingers. "That's ... too bad, kid."

Rocco shrugged.

"OK, then, who will be my second volunteer?" Enzo boomed.

Suddenly my right hand shot up in the air. "WAHHH!" I wailed, twisting round, to find that Posh Chloe was holding my arm up and waving it about. "Let go! No!"

"Yes, you! Young man!" Enzo shouted over to me.

No, no, no, I did *not* want to be onstage. "I made a mistake!" I shouted back.

"What's your name, young man?" Enzo replied.

"OTIS BUM-BUM!" Posh Chloe shouted, on my behalf.

"No!" I tried to say, but my wails were dwarfed by the laughter of the crowd.

"Up you come, OTIS BUM-BUM!" Enzo declared.

I shook my head, but then everyone started chanting, "OTIS! OTIS!" and some people started banging their hands on tables and stamping their feet, and it wasn't in a good way. I scowled at Posh Chloe, who gave me an evil grin in return, as I pushed through the crowd towards the stage to join Rocco. It's not that I'm afraid of hypnotists; my aunt went to see a hypnotist once to cure her fear of flying, and not only did she get on a plane to Las Vegas two months later, she got on that plane with the hypnotist and they got married out there, so I knew hypnosis could be, in my aunt's words, "The best thing to happen to a tired, middle-aged woman who feared life was behind her and just wanted one last shot at happiness". I just didn't want to end up doing anything humiliating that would make it any more unlikely I'd find a replacement Jagger. The look on Jack Jones' face, who was already filming all this from his spot at the front of the stage, told me this was probably going to be super embarrassing and I wasn't going to be allowed to forget any of it for a very long time.

"Look into my eyes!" Enzo said, as we got started.

Ugh. *How original.* It was going to be a long night.

Pretty soon, Enzo made me "fall asleep" although, actually, I was still awake – I was just playing along. Then he made me pretend I was stuck to my chair (although I could have got up if I'd wanted to), and finally he made me think I was a slug who was crawling along the stage on my way to a tasty vegetable patch – although, again, I was just going along with it to get it all done with as soon as possible. And it worked, because no sooner was I up there than it was all over. I gave a small nod to the applauding crowd, hopped off the stage, and made my way back towards Jagger.

"You. Were. *Sensational!*" Jagger beamed.

"Thanks," I said. "Come on, let's get away from here in case I'm volunteered to be on stage again. Fancy hanging round the chocolate fountain before trying out the fairground?"

"Remember what your mum said about too much sugar!" Jagger warned.

"Is my mum here?" I said.

Jagger shook his head.

"Are you my mum?"

"I don't think so," Jagger said.

"Are any of the people in this tent my mum?"

"Not as far as I know."

"THEN LET US DRINK FROM THE FOUNTAIN OF CHOCOLATE GOODNESS!" I yelled. I don't know why I yelled. I think I was losing the plot a bit because of all the sadness about Jagger mixed with all the excitement of being onstage.

I scampered over to the chocolate fountain, dipping strawberries, bananas and marshmallows as fast as I could. I just couldn't get enough chocolate. The trouble was, it actually took quite a long time to pick up, say, a mini pretzel, dip it in chocolate, and then eat it. I needed a bigger hit. So I grabbed an empty plastic beaker, filled it with melted chocolate, and downed it in one.

"MMMMMmmmmmm!" I cooed. "Oh, yeah, that hits the spot."

Jagger was looking at me with wide, concerned eyes.

I wiped my mouth with the back of my hand. "More," I said, scooping up another cupful.

"Wait!" Jagger said, grabbing my hand before the cup reached my mouth. "Is this wise?"

I hiccupped. "This is ... possibly ... the wisest ... *hiccup* ... thing I've ever done in my whole eleven years on this ... miserable planet."

I downed the chocolate.

"Besides," I added, "what do you care? You're LEAVING ME, YOU MONSTER!" I howled, repeating the words I'd heard my dad yell at my mum before he went to live in a Premier Inn on the outskirts of Basingstoke for five months.

"OK," Jagger said, probably knowing it was best to ignore my hysterics (because best friends know all about you, *sob!*), "there's a game of Sardines happening in a few minutes. Wanna play?"

"What's ... *hiccup* ... Sardines?"

"It's like hide and seek. One person hides, and the other people look for them, but if they find them, they have to join them and hide too. *Plus*, there's a Rocco twist, because he's hidden iPhones for people to find and keep. *And* team games are a good way of making new friends!"

New friends ... *new friends*... I just wanted to blank the whole concept out.

"Look!" I said. "I can put my whole hand in the chocolate fountain and..." I put my hand in, then slowly withdrew it. "Now I've got a chocolate hand!" I started licking it off. "Dream come true. Whole hand. Made of ... *hiccup* ... chocolate."

"Come and play Sardines," Jagger said.

"Go." I waved him away, accidentally flicking him with chocolate. "Maybe I'll make some friends right here and I will see you ... *mmmm, chocolate* ... later, and we'll ... *hiccup* ... and ... just going to have another slurp of this and then ... maybe some ... more."

"OK," Jagger said. "But come and play in a few minutes. And, um ... go easy on the chocolate."

I think he may have looked at me, waiting for my answer perhaps, but I was gurgling like a baby as I drizzled molten chocolate straight down my throat from the cup.

I'm not sure if I believe in heaven, but I think if there is such a place, it will be like having your entire head inside a chocolate fountain.

And next thing I knew … I was being hauled away from my precious chocolate fountain because apparently it's not acceptable to strip down to your boxers and attempt to swim in said fountain.

"But I've brought spare pants!" I shouted to the assembled crowd as Tiana (the G.O.A.T – major year six celeb!) dragged me off.

"You've had too much sugar, mate!" Tiana told me, as she bundled me back into my clothes and wiped my face with a napkin.

I looked up at her. *So tall.* "I have had … nowhere near enough! Barely a teaspoon of sugar has passed these lips!" I said, craning my neck up. "LET'S DANCE, SHALL WE DANCE?!"

And I ran off to the dance floor where the DJ was dropping some funky *beatz*.

Yeah, *beatz* with a *z* because that's how funky they were!

Mounted a podium.

Did my famous crocodile-peacock-charging-bull dance.

Snap! Snap! Shake your tail feathers! Horn! Horn! Paw

the ground… CHARGING BULL!

Combo of amazing dance moves plus flames disco shirt equals cheering from crowd.

"What is he doing?" someone said, their voice full of admiration, I'm sure. "Do we need to call an ambulance?"

Hahahahahaha! I was just fine.

More than fine.

The lights, the music, I was alive, I was buzzing,

I was ninety per cent chocolate and that is a very amazing thing to be. There would be a *waiting list* of people wanting to be my friend by the end of *this* night!

As I threw myself off the podium to crowd-surf back towards the chocolate fountain, I knew the truth.

That I was ... EPIC.

(And I needed more sugar).

CHAPTER 7
SLEEPOVER TAKEOVER

The sound of chirping birds and a soft, gentle breeze on my face brought me round from a deep, deep sleep the following morning. *Wow*, that must have been some party. I yawned and stretched, and my eyelids fluttered open ... which is when I realized the "gentle breeze" was in fact an ACTUAL LIVE DONKEY breathing over my face. I stared at it, frozen and wide-eyed. What on earth?!

The donkey grinned, displaying his full set of gnashers, then licked me.

"Ugh! Gross!" I squealed, trying to roll

away from under the beast's massive head.

But I couldn't roll.

I couldn't really move at all.

It was like I was trapped under a really heavy blanket. A really heavy, puffy white blanket that didn't want me to sit or stand up.

"Gah!" I mumbled, as I twisted left, then right, basically beached like a whale, under this huge— Oh, but hang on, I wasn't *under* it … I was *in* it. I was … wearing it? I was wearing this thing, because it was a … WEDDING DRESS?

I was wearing a wedding dress.

I was wearing a wedding dress, I'd just been kissed by a donkey, and hovering just above my head was a GIANT INFLATABLE SAUSAGE.

I rubbed my eyes. Maybe this was a dream? A sugar-induced dream. A hallucination, perhaps?

I blinked it all away … until the donkey's grinning face came back into focus. Then he made an ear-shattering *HEE-HAW!* noise, *winked* at me, like I was his girlfriend, and sauntered off to lick up the remains of the chocolate fountain.

My mouth felt very dry and my head hurt a bit. I tried to think back to the party last night. I remembered having some chocolate ... and some more chocolate... I remembered dancing, and then... I tried to steady my breathing. I couldn't remember anything after the dancing. It was blank. Why was I in a wedding dress? Why was there an inflatable sausage above my head? What was a donkey doing in here?!

"What has happened?" I muttered to myself.

"WHAT HAS HAPPENED?!" a voice screamed.

I twisted myself around, still unable to stand for all the dress I was cocooned in, and saw Rocco, in his gold satin, monogrammed pyjamas, jumping about in rage in the centre of the marquee. "Look at all this mess!" he squealed. "It's WRECKED! Who let that donkey in? GET IT OUT! Why is there a giant sausage? Half the people here are VEGAN! ARGH!" He stomped over to me, kicking at my dress. *"What are you wearing?"*

I opened and closed my mouth several times, but I couldn't make any words come out. It was only then, once he'd come closer to me, that I saw he had something written on his forehead. Actually, not so much *written* as … possibly *tattooed*. In big letters:

LOSER.

"What are you staring at?" Rocco demanded.

"Um … nothing," I replied, thinking it best not to say or do anything that might anger him any further. I looked around for Jagger, hoping he would be able to help me get out of this enormous – but still quite slimming – dress, but he wasn't anywhere to be seen. *Huh*.

By this time, after all of Rocco's shouting, everyone else was awake, and that's when things got even weirder.

"Who left this here?" Tiana asked, holding up a garden ornament of a peeing cherub.

The peeing cherub, which was probably part of a pond display, was about half a metre tall and made of concrete, in the form of a small boy with curly hair, having a wee. Except, this peeing cherub was missing an important part of his anatomy, which appeared to have snapped or broken off.

"He's lost his winkle," I muttered.

"His *winkle*?!" Rocco scoffed. "*Winkle*?! What are you, five?"

"Should we look for it?" Tiana asked, examining

the stricken boy.

"Put it down!" Rocco shouted, just as the donkey, who had been licking the chocolate fountain with real gusto, licked a bit too hard, and the whole contraption toppled over, spilling a lake of liquid chocolate all over the floor. "ARGH! MY PARENTS ARE GOING TO KILL ME!"

I saw Tiana squint at the letters tattooed on Rocco's forehead. "Rocco, why have you got—" she began, just as I shook my head at her to stop talking. I didn't think Rocco needed anything else to be upset about right now.

"Why have I got *what?*" Rocco demanded.

"Why have you got a suitcase full of sausages?" Posh Chloe replied, coming forward with an open case, stuffed full of bratwurst. "This is really freaky, Rocco!" she added. She looked at him, and I saw her also clock what was written on his forehead. "Um, Rocco—"

"Which of you did all this? HUH?" Rocco was now red with rage. "My parents are gonna ground me! They'll never let me have a party again! I promised them it would all be OK! That was the deal! At first they didn't want to let me because of Coco's party last year, which got leaked on TikTok and two thousand people turned

85

up and trashed the place! 'That won't happen to me!' I said! 'I'm a good, responsible boy!' I said! AND NOW LOOK! When my parents see this … this … this…"

"Apocalypse?" I murmured, still beached on the ground, and feeling really *weird*, like a bit dizzy and woozy. "Rocco-apoca-lypse…" I glanced around for Jagger, who I knew would appreciate my little bit of hilarious wordplay, but he was still nowhere to be seen.

"SHUT UP!" Rocco howled. "But, also, yes! This apocalypse! When my parents see it, they'll go ballistic. They'll go nuclear! My mother especially cannot stand any sort of mess or clutter." He shook his head. "She's a devout minimalist. She's in a book club with Marie Kondo."

I blew out a breath. It all seemed very serious.

Rocco was pacing about. "One of you did this!" He breathed heavily, glaring at everyone's stunned faces. "One of you is responsible! And when I find out who…"

"HEE-HAW!" went the donkey, as he rolled on his back and slathered himself in the chocolate lake, which was slowly seeping in my direction.

"Oh my god," Rocco muttered.

Other Chloe bent down to a large crate on the floor,

which had holes drilled in its sides and *Live animals: handle with care!* stamped on it. "What's in here?" she asked, prising off the lid before I had a chance to suggest that probably wouldn't be the best move.

And, what do you know? No sooner as the lid was off than a flock of WHITE DOVES flew out and started darting and dive-bombing all around the marquee.

"Argh! It's a plague of bats!" Rocco screamed, covering his head.

"Doves!" I corrected him.

"Whatever, one's just pooed on me!" he squealed. "ARGH!"

The marquee was soon filled with the screams of my peers as Jake, Jack and Jon, and the Chloes, and the Drama Darlings, the chess club, Tiana, and all the other guests dived and darted, trying to avoid the wild, pooing doves. Meanwhile, all the commotion must have scared the donkey because he made several loud *HEE-HAW!* noises, scrambled up, slipped and slid through the chocolate lake, before bolting through to the other marquee and jumping in the ball pit, sending the contents flying everywhere. Rocco turned to see what new calamity was happening

and stepped forward, only to put his foot down on one of the balls, his legs flying up from underneath him, as he smacked down in a pool of chocolate and, aided by his shiny pyjamas, slid at high speed all the way over to me, where my soft wedding dress cushioned the impact, as he came to a rest, his head on my tummy.

As the doves all eventually found the exit and made their escape, so too did all of Rocco's guests, one by one, making their excuses, or just wandering off to call their parents for an early lift home, none of them wanting to be held responsible, or in any way involved in sorting out whatever had gone on here last night.

Every single one of them.

All gone.

Until it was just me and Rocco, still lying in a pool of chocolate on the floor.

Rocco was staring up at the ceiling, silent.

"I know this all seems really bad," I said, after a bit, "but just so you know, and are in full possession of all the facts … you also have the word '*loser*' tattooed on your forehead. But I'm sure everything will be fine."

Rocco burst into tears.

CHAPTER 8
DONKEEEEEEY!

"There, there." I patted Rocco on the shoulder, as he sniffed and wiped his eyes. "Maybe it's one of those temporary ones?"

Rocco vigorously rubbed his thumb over his forehead. "Gone?"

"No. But hey, I hear laser removal of tattoos is quite good now, and while it may be a bit painful, it hardly leaves any scarring."

Rocco's bottom lip started to wobble again, before he took a deep, forceful breath and glared at me. *"You,"* he snarled.

"Me, *what?*"

"*You* did this. All of this! Of course you did!"

I laughed out loud, because that was the most ridiculous thing I'd ever heard. "Rocco, I may not be able to remember most of last night, but I do know I have no reason to ruin your birthday sleepover."

"OK, first off, it wasn't just a 'birthday sleepover'," Rocco said. "It was a glamorous ball in celebration of the anniversary of my birth. Second, of course you had reason to ruin it: jealousy!"

"What do I have to be jealous of?" I asked, looking at the gorgeous, handsome, popular boy standing in the midst of a huge birthday marquee that was sitting in the grounds of his multi-million-pound home. "I'm very happy as I am, thanks."

Rocco narrowed his eyes at me. "OK. Then you're angry and bitter about the fact you weren't even meant to be here!"

"You invited me!"

"I didn't! Or at least, I didn't want to!"

"Then why am I here?"

"Because my dad parked his SUV literally for five seconds outside the artisan delicatessen and *your mum*

gave him a ticket! She was really unreasonable about it all, and only agreed to let him off if I gave you and Jagger an invite to the party she'd heard about on the parents' WhatsApp group!"

I swallowed. Mum *was* an enthusiastic member of the parents' WhatsApp group, and she *was* keen for me to make new friends. Even so, my mum? Bend the rules around traffic? This sounded unlikely. Maybe Rocco was just saying this to try to hurt my feelings, because he was angry?

"I don't believe you," I said.

"Whether or not you believe me is irrelevant!" Rocco hissed. "It's the truth, so deal with it! You weren't meant to be here, and I bet you knew that in your heart of hearts, and to get me back, you ruined my whole party."

"What, by stealing a donkey and putting a wedding dress on?"

Rocco glared at me.

I sighed. I *did* know that it was odd being invited to his party. That was why I was so suspicious all night – I couldn't work it out. Now it was clear: it all came down to a parking fine. I kicked myself for being so stupid and thinking maybe I belonged here, and that one of them would ever want to be my replacement friend, when in reality I was just a dork who no one wanted around.

"That dress isn't terrible, by the way," Rocco muttered.

I looked down at it, unsure how to respond. "Thank you?"

"It needs taking in a bit..."

"I feel like the neckline could be lower..."

"Mmm, yes," Rocco agreed. "But stop trying to distract me! You clearly went on some sort of wild escapade, creating as much chaos and mess as possible in the hope of getting me in trouble!"

"Well, that certainly doesn't sound like me, but I can't remember anything," I said.

"Really? Well, isn't that convenient!" Rocco replied, giving me a very sarcastic smile.

"OK, well what do *you* remember?" I asked. "If I was getting up to so much trouble, *when* was I doing it? Tell me! You were here all night, weren't you?"

"Yes!" Rocco snapped.

"Well?" I waited.

Rocco breathed heavily. "I don't know," he said,

finally. "My mind is kind of blank after about nine o'clock."

"So you're telling me you can't remember either?"

Rocco shrugged. "It doesn't matter because *the criminal*," he pointed at me, "is plain for all to see!"

I closed my eyes and groaned. If Rocco had decided I was to blame, that was it for me. Rocco was basically a god. I had ruined a god's birthday ball. I knew my Percy Jackson: I was headed for eternal torment in the underworld … otherwise known as being a friendless year seven in secondary school.

At this point we heard footsteps outside the marquee and a woman's voice called out, "Yoo-hoo! Rocco, darling!"

"My mum!" Rocco rasped, his eyes wide with panic. "Oh no, oh god, it's all over now! I promised them there would be no trouble! I'll be grounded for *months!* They'll stop my allowance until the cleaning bills are paid off, I'll be banished from our luxury yacht, and Coco will revel in my downfall! What am I going to do?"

"How should I know?"

Rocco glared at me again. "Well … think of

something! I can't go out there with *loser* tattooed on my forehead!" And he manhandled me up to a standing position and towards the exit, then shoved me through the big tinsel glitter curtain that hung across the entrance.

I stumbled right into a tall, glamorous woman wearing a kaftan, who must have been Rocco's mum; a slightly shorter man, wearing what looked like some kind of baggy Tai Chi suit, who must have been his dad; and his sister, Coco, just as they arrived.

"Good morning!" I trilled, sweeping

the veil, which had dropped down in front of my face, back over my head.

Mrs Rococo looked me up and down in my dress, and smiled at me. "Well, don't you look lovely?"

"Thank you, Ma'aaaaaaaaaaam!" I bleated, while doing a curtsey. "Just a little something I threw on quickly!"

No one laughed. *Tough crowd.*

"We were just coming to see if you kids wanted some breakfast?" Mr Rococo said. "Although it seems a lot of you have headed home early. OK if we come in?"

I barred his way. "No!"

"No?" He frowned. "Why not?"

I chewed my lip while I thought about it. "Because ... because Rocco, who is very kind and thoughtful" – *what a lie!* – "wanted to surprise you by making sure the marquee is lovely and tidy first." I nodded, while the Rococo family looked back at me, blankly. "Oh, er, not that there's loads of mess or anything, or—"

"HEE-HAW!"

"What was that?" Mrs Rococo said, trying to peer around me and through the glitter curtain.

"What was what? I didn't hear anything."

"HEE-HAW!"

"*That!*" Mrs Rococo repeated.

"Oh! Oh, *that!*" I said. "That's ... that's ... that is Posh Chloe, one of the Chloes, that's her, um... She has this *problem.*" I lowered my voice. "*Flatulence.*" I screwed up my face. "It's pretty icky and she's very embarrassed about it."

Mrs Rococo shook her head. "Poor girl."

"Yes," I agreed. "It's pretty impossible to hide your farts when they sound like a donkey."

"HEE-HAW!"

"There she goes again! Old Parpy-Pants!" I smiled politely.

"Can we talk to Rocco, at least?" Mrs Rococo asked, moving forwards.

I put my arms out to stop her. "No, no! He's on his knees ... scrubbing and cleaning, and refuses to come out until it's all done!"

Coco rolled her eyes. "Ugh. He's such a loser."

"Is he, now?" I asked, eyes suddenly narrowing in her direction. A vindictive older sister with a taste for tattooing? She already told us she resented Rocco and his friends being here last night. What lengths might she go to, to get revenge?

Mr Rococo crossed his arms. "He's a growing boy, he must want breakfast! ROCCO? DO YOU WANT BREAKFAST?" he hollered over my shoulder.

"No-oh!" came Rocco's shaky, strained voice, in reply. "Sit down, you stupid thing! Thank you, no breakfast! Argh! Get off my foot!"

"He's fine for breakfast," I told them.

"But we have smoked salmon and scrambled eggs!" Mrs Rococo said.

"Smoked salmon and scrambled eggs, Rocco?" I shouted back.

"Stop licking my face!" came Rocco's reply.

"Ha!" I told an alarmed-looking Rococo family. "Some of our classmates have a lot to learn about personal boundaries. Luckily, Rocco is a patient teacher. AREN'T YOU, ROCCO?"

"Oh my god, he's just pooed everywhere!" Rocco shouted back.

I gave an apologetic smile to the Rococos. "He is, of course, talking about our friend, Jagger, who may have overindulged on the barbecued prawns and is now afflicted with a terrible case of the uncontrollable poops... Oh! Um ... not that Rocco meant he's pooed *everywhere*, and definitely not in the tent, more ... in the emergency bucket that's been provided, which also sounds gross, so I'll stop now, but just to absolutely reassure you, there is no poop in the marquee."

I nodded, like this was all fine. Although, actually, speaking of Jagger, where on earth was he? I hadn't seen him once since I woke up. Then again, it was pretty chaotic, so maybe he just ran off in the mayhem? I probably would have done that too, if I'd actually been able to move in this dress.

Mrs Rococo sighed. "OK, well, we'll leave some food out in the kitchen if you kids get hungry. I'd completely forgotten we'd won a family trip to a yoga retreat today, so we're all heading off, but I'm sure you'll all be fine by yourselves, you're all fifteen after all!"

"Eleven. We're eleven."

"Play with knives and fire."

I squinted at her. "Was there meant to be a 'don't' in that sentence?"

She ignored me, glanced over my shoulder again and called out, "It's so … *unusual* of you to want to help clean up, Rocco, but I'm very proud of you. It's a very thoughtful gesture, even though we could just get some of the staff to do it on Monday."

There was silence, but instead of a response from Rocco, all we heard was a galloping sound and an "OHHHHHH NOOOOOOOO!" from inside.

Sensing the galloping was getting closer, I hedged my bets, pointed behind the Rococos and shouted, "LOOK, WHAT'S THAT?" just as Rocco flew through the glitter curtain on the back of the bucking donkey, which, seemingly frightened by the sight of me in my wedding dress, immediately lurched back inside the depths of the marquee just as his family turned back around. "Sorry, I thought it was … Superman," I explained. "But it was just a bird." I cracked a smile. "Or was it a plane?"

Another great joke that no one laughed at!

"OK, dear," Mrs Rococo sighed. "Let's make a move. It's lucky I remembered about the yoga retreat – I so desperately need to reconnect with my chakras!"

"Have fun!" I said, as Mr and Mrs Rococo, and Coco, meandered off for their day of luxury.

With the coast clear, I pushed back through the glitter curtain to find Rocco sitting, breathless, in the middle of the floor and the donkey stepping unsteadily through all the overturned food carts, sampling all the leftovers.

"The donkey's high on sugar!" Rocco gasped. "He's out of control. How did you ever get him in here?"

I put my hands on my hips. "This again! How many times? I didn't do any of this!"

"Well, why would any of my real friends do this?" he retorted.

"If I wanted to get you in trouble, why did I cover for you in front of your parents? Why, if I was the person who did this, would I stick around? That doesn't make any sense."

I watched as Rocco thought about it too, chewing his lip. Eventually, he looked back up at me and sniffed. "You're right."

"Thank you."

"We're looking for someone who made a clean

getaway," Rocco said.

"Right!" I agreed.

"But someone – like you – who has reason to dislike me."

"Maybe!" I said.

"Someone who perhaps enjoys pranks; who maybe has a reputation for them?"

I shrugged. "Well…"

Rocco narrowed his eyes. *"So where's Jagger?"*

CHAPTER 9
POISONOUS MONSTER BUG
(PROBABLY)

"He's still not picking up." I sighed, putting down Rocco's phone. Mum had promised me my own phone when I got to secondary school, but it's lucky that Mr Banerjee made us memorize important phone numbers "in the event of a state-sponsored hacking attack" during one of our survival classes. My memorized numbers were Jagger, Mum and the pizza parlour.

Rocco crossed his arms, towering over me. "So!" he said. "Jagger disappears, nowhere to be seen, he's not taking calls... I think we have our culprit!"

"Innocent until proven guilty!" I reminded him.

"Challenge accepted!" Rocco retorted. "He's always pranking people. It's a foregone conclusion that he's responsible for all this."

I sighed again. I didn't think for one minute that Jagger was behind all this; it just didn't make sense. He was excited about the party. He kept telling *me* not to worry and that I should just try to enjoy it – he wanted *me* to make new friends, because he cared about me. Why would he try to sabotage that?

And yet a feeling still nagged in my stomach. Where was he, then? Why hadn't Jagger stuck around? Me and Jagger did everything together. We looked out for one another. *Always had, always will.* There had to be an explanation.

I certainly wasn't going to let Rocco accuse him of stuff that I felt sure he wouldn't have done. Someone was going to have to stand up for him, and that someone was going to have to be me.

"Listen," I said, hauling myself to my feet so I was facing Rocco. "Something clearly happened here last night."

"Oh, *you think?*" Rocco replied, incredulously.

I ignored his sarcastic tone. "Something happened, and we can argue and throw accusations around, then I'll just go home, you'll get in trouble with your parents, and everyone will be sad, especially you ... *or* we can try to sort it all out."

I swallowed, and tried my best to look confident. But the truth was, I was winging it. I had no idea how we'd sort all this out.

Rocco held my gaze, took a deep breath, and slowly exhaled. "Fine," he said, finally. "But this had better not all be part of some plan to make things even worse for me."

"You can trust me."

"Ha!" Rocco said. "I only trust my friends. You're not my friend."

I nodded, not taking my eyes off him. "You mean the 'friends' who all ran off home at the first hint of trouble?"

Rocco frowned, and looked down at the floor. For a fleeting moment, he didn't look his usual, confident self, and for the first time, I actually felt a bit sorry for him. "They probably had stuff to do," he muttered.

"OK, well, first things first, I need to change out of this dress," I said.

"Oh? Almost seems a shame," Rocco said.

"Yeah, it does have a great silhouette, but it's hardly practical when we have all this to sort out. It's OK," I said. "I have a change of clothes in my bag."

Rocco nodded, and I scooted off to the cloakroom area to grab my stuff. Unfortunately, all the clothes in my bag were covered in sticky chocolate. I had *no idea* how that happened, but clearly I was involved in *something* last night. Did I have more to do with all this than even I knew? Either way, I decided this would not be a good thing to mention to Rocco, as it might make me look even more guilty.

"Changed my mind!" I trilled, when I returned to Rocco. "I thought about it, and actually, this dress *is* sensational. I'll, um ... keep it on. Unless you've ... got anything different you could maybe ... lend me?"

"I haven't," Rocco said bluntly.

I nodded. "Great! Because I love this dress, so, that's ... really perfect."

"Great," Rocco replied.

"Although," I added, "it does appear to have a rather unfortunate stain around the back – from when I was lying in the pool of chocolate earlier." I lowered my voice. "It kind of looks like I've had an *accident*."

"Yes, it does," Rocco agreed, offering no further solutions to my dilemma.

I nodded. "Great! Because I love being humiliated, so that's also … really perfect."

"Great," Rocco replied.

I gritted my teeth, swallowed back my annoyance at how moody and unhelpful Rocco was being, and we set to work. While Rocco went to get changed out of his gold pyjamas, I borrowed his phone again to call my mum and let her know I was hanging out with him for the day.

"That's *great*, Otis, that means I can take an extra shift – I've got a fresh batch of fixed penalty notices I'm just dying to crack open!" she said.

After absolutely ages, Rocco returned wearing some grey Armani joggers, a white Moschino T-shirt, Ray Ban's, a Hugo Boss manbag, and a modest pair of white Versace trainers, studded with diamonds, having also showered, done his hair, and "filed his nails because one was a bit rough". We decided the best plan would be to collect all the weird stuff in the marquee, try to work out where it had come from, and then return it. In the process, we would hopefully be able to find out what on earth happened last night and *who* was really responsible. With Jagger not being around in September, the last thing I needed was to incur the wrath of Rocco, who would doubtless spread it around the school that I was some sort of bitter, party-ruining scumbag who should regularly have his trousers removed and be gaffer-taped to goalposts for the amusement of the popular kids.

I told Rocco to fetch a wheelbarrow so we could load everything in it.

"What's a wheelbarrow?" he asked.

I stared at him. "A wheelbarrow! It's a... How can you not know what a wheelbarrow is?! You use it in the garden!"

Rocco shrugged. "We have gardeners."

I blinked at him in disbelief. Being rich was another world! "Right. Well, a wheelbarrow is a ... barrow, with a ... wheel!" I explained.

Rocco seemed to understand, went away while I started collecting up all the weird stuff, and then came back, moments later, empty-handed.

"Couldn't find one?" I asked.

Rocco shook his head. "No. I mean, yes, I found one."

"So where is it?"

Rocco looked shifty. "There was some kind of poisonous monster bug on it."

I flicked my eyes to his. "Really?"

Rocco nodded.

"Let's see," I said.

Rocco led the way around the back of the marquee and over towards a far corner of his massive garden, where there was a compost heap, a greenhouse, and yes, the wheelbarrow. He stood back as I approached it with caution.

"Poisonous monster bug?" I said.

"Can you see it?" he wailed.

"It's a woodlouse." I brushed the critter away, grabbed the wheelbarrow, and pushed it past an open-mouthed Rocco, back towards the marquee.

I had a feeling it was going to be a long day.

We loaded the suitcase of bratwurst, the peeing cherub with the missing winkle, and the empty wooden crate into the wheelbarrow, and tied the giant inflatable sausage to one of the handles. Meanwhile, using a spare length of rope that hadn't been used for the marquee, we managed to tether the donkey so one of us could lead the thing behind the wheelbarrow.

I scanned the marquee for any remaining things that seemed out of place. "Hmm," I said. "What about these?" I held up four random-looking outfits: a police officer, workman dungarees with a yellow hard hat, a cowboy and a sailor.

"So those are definitely weird, they look like fancy dress costumes," Rocco said. "Put them in the barrow with a wheel and handles."

"Just 'wheelbarrow' is fine, Rocco."

"*Wheel-barrow*," he repeated, like he was trying to get used to the word.

I slung the fancy dress costumes in. "Right! So, do any of these items look familiar in any way? Any clues? We just need to work out where they all came from, retrace our steps, and—"

"I need a break," Rocco said, sitting down and fanning his face.

"Why don't we have some of the breakfast your mum left?" I suggested. "And we can get started after that?"

"Mmm, I'm not hungry, though."

"Really? I thought you just told your parents that to get them off our backs?"

Rocco shook his head. "No, I'm weirdly full. I guess I must have eaten a lot last night, although I can't..."

"Really remember?"

Rocco nodded and looked at me. "Why can't we remember anything?"

"I've no idea," I said. "That's something we've got to find out." I sighed and glanced at the contents of the wheelbarrow, eyes alighting on the peeing cherub with the missing winkle. I suddenly remembered something we had talked about at school on Friday – the witch who lived near me, who had a garden full of gnomes! This peeing cherub with the missing winkle was *exactly* the sort of monstrosity she would have in her garden! I couldn't be sure, but it was the best lead we had right now.

"Come on!" I told Rocco.

"Wait!" Rocco squealed. "I can't go anywhere! I've got a terrible word tattooed on my forehead!" Rocco lay down on the ground, the back of his hand to his head. "I am doomed to live a life of solitude."

I frisbeed the sailor hat to him. "Whack this on!" I told him. "And pull it down over your head a bit so it covers it up."

He frowned at the hat, then pulled it on his head.

"There!" I said. "Very fetching."

"Don't try to flatter me – I know your game!" Rocco grumbled. "So, where are we going?"

"To see the witch!"

Rocco rolled his eyes and shrugged, and I had to chuckle to myself as we left the marquee, because that's a boy who's scared of woodlice, but not actual witches.

Although I wasn't laughing for long…

CHAPTER 10
THE PEEING CHERUB WITH THE MISSING WINKLE

As we strolled through town on our way to the witch's house, I guess I hadn't accounted for how much attention we would attract. Thinking about it, a boy in a wedding dress pushing a wheelbarrow with a huge inflatable sausage attached, followed by a boy dressed top-to-toe in designer gear and … a sailor's cap, leading a donkey, probably isn't something most people see every day.

"Gorgeous dress!" a woman said, smiling as she passed us.

"Congratulations!" a man shouted from his car,

giving me a thumbs up. "Although I think you may have *sat* in something!"

I was worried all of this would embarrass Rocco and put him in even more of a bad mood – the last thing I needed if I was going to be spending most of the day with him, sorting this mess out. So, I tried to distract him with some chat. "I wonder what happened to the peeing cherub's winkle?" I said.

"Someone must have dropped him at some point," Rocco said. "And his winkle must have broken off."

I winced. "Ouch!"

For the first time that day, Rocco actually laughed. "But this little dude is made from concrete, so I don't suppose he cares."

The person who *would* care, of course, was the witch (whose name in the neighbourhood was Sally Hopkins, but this was clearly a lie because that's not a witch's name; I'd no doubt she was *really* called Cruella Wart, or similar). The witch was well known for being very protective about her gnomes, and the notion that one had been stolen would have sent her spiralling. If she'd already discovered it was missing, of course. And assuming it *did* belong to her. (And, thinking about it, if the gnome was actually a child who "had moved away", the winkle situation maybe really did hurt.)

Rocco and I hatched a plan: check her back garden to see if she had a pond, and if she did, check to see if there was an obvious spot where a peeing cherub would stand, and, if so, quickly put it back and scarper. She would then eventually discover the peeing cherub, notice his winkle was missing, but wouldn't know how it happened or that we had anything to do with it. Simple.

Or so we thought.

Turning the corner, the witch's house loomed into view. Unlike your traditional witch, who might reside in a sinister thatched cottage with twisted, gnarly trees outside, surrounded by mist, with the smell of freshly cooking bones wafting around, Sally (*if she was really called that!*) lived in a small new-build semi with net curtains and a sign on the front door that read:

YOU DON'T HAVE
TO BE MAD
TO LIVE HERE –
BUT IT HELPS!

But this was clearly all a ruse to throw witch-hunters off the scent.

"Oh no!" Rocco suddenly grabbed me. "Look! Across the road from her house!"

My eyes widened. *A police car.* "We don't know whether that's there because of her," I said, just as her front door opened and an actual policeman stepped outside. "Ohhhh! Hide! Hide!" I babbled.

"How are we meant to hide with a donkey?!"

"Gah! Good point!" I took a deep breath and tried to think about what Jagger would do. Jagger ... who was so into his pranks and tricks ... how would he make something disappear? "We need to act normal and not attract suspicion..." I thought aloud, well aware that, along with the donkey, I was in a wedding dress, we had a giant, inflatable sausage floating above us, and we were in possession of the stolen item Sally had probably just spoken to the police about. Pretty hard to blend in ... so if you can't blend in, maybe it's best just to be obvious...?

I grinned to myself, remembering. Jagger and I once discussed (in a scary amount of detail considering we weren't serious) how best to commit a diamond heist and then get the gems out of the country. Our solution? You get them out in a van marked:

No one would believe anyone would be that stupid.

"Shouldn't we just turn around and get out of here?" Rocco suggested.

I shook my head. "Hurrying away from the scene of a crime? Us lot? Like this? Wedding dress, donkey and giant sausage? Rookie error! It's bound to attract that policeman's attention, and if he comes over, he'll find the cherub! Sometimes it's best to hide in plain sight."

Rocco didn't look convinced.

"Look," I said, keeping one eye on where the policeman was. "If you were a burglar, but you didn't want anyone to really believe you were a burglar, what would you wear? What would be the best disguise?"

"I dunno," Rocco shrugged. "Like, dark clothes, maybe a mask? A hoodie?"

I shook my head. "A black-and-white striped top and a bag with *SWAG* written on it."

Rocco's eyes lit up. "Like a cartoon burglar outfit! No one would really think you were one because no one really thinks burglars look like that! Crooks always try to hide, so be obvious – deliberately stand out! Hide in plain sight!"

"You got it!" I gestured towards the bus stop that was across the road from the police car. "Now come on!"

And so we all lined up at the bus stop, a proud bunch of weirdos.

The plan worked, because even when the policeman

looked at us with astonishment, I just waved and smiled, and acted like it was all fine. And in return, he smiled back! I guess, sometimes, you've just gotta wear your weirdness with pride; it's when you try to hide it the problems start.

The policeman got back in his patrol car and made a radio call to base, which we were luckily just close enough to hear through his open window:

"Suspected theft of stone ornament in the form of a urinating cherub," the policeman said. "Victim witnessed suspect in the vicinity last night – IC1 female, approximately eleven years of age, wearing a distinctive headdress in the form of two bendy springs with pom-poms on the end."

Once the police car had driven off, I turned to Rocco, who was staring straight ahead, breathing heavily. "Other Chloe!" he hissed. "It was her all along!"

"OK, but hang on," I said. "I know the headdress thing makes her seem guilty, but what if she was framed?"

Rocco shook his head. "Nah. It all makes sense. She's always been the odd one out. Never quite fitted in with

Posh Chloe and Sporty Chloe. All this time, she was just waiting for her chance to bring me down, plotting, scheming..."

"OK, well, I think it's only fair to give her a chance to explain her side of the—"

"No way!" Rocco said, stomping off down the street, pulling the donkey behind him. "We're going round to her house now, we're going to perform a citizen's arrest and we're going to see that girl thrown in jail for a *very* long time!"

"Oh, jeez," I sighed, grabbing the wheelbarrow and hurrying after him.

CHAPTER 11
WAR HORSE

"Careful, you'll break it down!" I told Rocco, as he hammered on Other Chloe's front door.

"I don't care, I'm so angry!" he replied. "I can't wait to see how she's going to try to worm her way out of this one!" He turned to me. "And don't start your 'innocent until proven guilty' nonsense again. She's been positively identified! *By a witch!*"

"Are witches reliable, though?"

"Of course they are!" Rocco snapped. "They've got magic on their side. And dark arts in general. *They know things.*"

Finally, the door opened, and a confused-looking

Other Chloe blinked at us. Her hair had been tied into two bunches, and she was wearing dungarees rather than her usual "The Chloes" pinafore dress. She almost looked, well, *normal*. "Otis?" she said. "Hello, Rocco."

But rather than launching into a tirade against her, I was slightly taken aback when, instead, Rocco did this: **BWARK! BWARK! BWARK! BWARK!**

Other Chloe stared at him. "What are you doing?"

I wanted to know that too. And, by the startled expression on his face, I'm not sure Rocco knew the answer.

"I'm ... being a chicken!" he said, finally. "Because ... because, that's what YOU are! A chicken!"

"Right?" Other Chloe said, looking totally confused.

"Yes!" Rocco continued. "You're a chicken for not telling me to my face that you don't like me! Instead, you've been sneaky, and you've plotted to ruin my birthday party. Well, congratulations! You nearly got away with it! Except you didn't, because I've discovered the truth, and now the jury – which is me – will give the verdict." He took a dramatic pause. "GUILTY as charged! TAKE HER DOWN!"

Nobody moved, and Rocco nudged me. "Take her down!" he hissed.

"Take her down *where*?" I replied.

"I don't know, that's what they say on TV!" Rocco said. He put his hands on his hips. "You sure made a quick exit from the marquee this morning! Got something to hide, have you?"

Other Chloe folded her arms and leaned against the doorframe. "My mum was due to pick me up anyway, and she couldn't park the car because of all the traffic restrictions on your road." She glanced at me in a pointed way. *"She didn't want to get clamped."*

"Ha! A likely story!" Rocco declared. "Couldn't wait to leave the scene of the crime, more like!"

This was all getting a bit too tense. "Look," I began, "do you know anything about the cherub from the tent, which apparently got stolen from the witch's house?"

"What? No!" Other Chloe said.

"She's lying," Rocco muttered.

I ignored him. "What about taking the donkey? Or the giant inflatable sausage? It's OK, we won't be cross" – I ignored Rocco's snort of indignation – "we just want to get to the bottom of all this."

"Honestly, I've no idea," Chloe replied.

"Lies!" Rocco said. "You were *seen*! Account for all your movements last night!"

Other Chloe looked blankly at us, and swallowed.

Rocco narrowed his eyes. "Gotcha!"

"It's not that, Rocco," Other Chloe said. "It's that … well, it's just, ever since I left your place this morning, I've been trying to think how it all happened, how all this random stuff got there and … I can't actually remember."

Something about this was starting to feel weird. "You too, huh?"

Other Chloe nodded. "I can remember the party up to a certain point, but then – total blank! And I'm guessing you two are in the same boat, otherwise you wouldn't have so many questions?"

I glanced at Rocco, who seemed to be grinding his teeth in either frustration or anger. "Come on, Rocco," I said. "Other Chloe wouldn't sabotage your party. She's your friend, isn't she?"

"So what if she's my friend?"

"Friends don't do that sort of thing."

Rocco laughed mockingly. "Yeah, they do."

"To be fair," Other Chloe said, "Posh Chloe and Sporty Chloe are mean to me all the time. They deliberately didn't tell me about the 'gold, frankincense and myrrh' thing for your present, so that I'd look foolish. Not that I'd have known where to get myrrh from anyway. What even is it?"

Rocco stared at her, sizing the situation up. "Well, I like Toblerone, so we're all good," he said. "But facts are facts, and the fact is the police are looking for you because a girl your height wearing pom-poms on her head, was seen *taking the cherub!*"

"But I don't remember doing that!" Other Chloe pleaded.

"Convenient!" Rocco said.

"Do you remember how you got that tattoo you're

trying to cover up?"

Rocco looked shifty and pulled his sailor's cap back down a bit. "Huh. Well … no."

"Otis?" Other Chloe turned her attention to me. "Remember how you ended up wearing that dress?"

"No idea." I sighed, pushing the veil, which kept falling over my eyes, back over my head again.

Other Chloe nodded. "Well … I could help you try to find out, if you like?"

Rocco narrowed his eyes. "What do you want in return?"

"Um … nothing?" Other Chloe said.

"But what's in it for you?" Rocco persisted.

Other Chloe shook her head. "Nothing, I guess? Except, if you say I was involved, then I should help you sort it out?"

I turned to Rocco, who shrugged back at me. "Great," I said. "I think we need all the help we can get."

"I wish I'd never worn those stupid pom-poms," Other Chloe muttered, as she pulled her shoes on.

"Then why did you?" Rocco asked. "Aha! Was it because a good way for criminals to get away with it is to hide in plain sight and be as obvious as possible? *We know your game, missy!*"

Other Chloe shook her head. "I was just sick of all the Chloes having to dress the same all the time. What's wrong with a bit of individuality?"

"Well, yeah," I said. "What *is* wrong with that?"

"Oh well, Posh Chloe doesn't like it. She says we're *a brand*, and that means all dressing the same. She was so furious I broke the rules last night – she threatened to expel me from the Chloes." Other Chloe nodded and sighed. "We're not supposed to do anything 'uncool', like be too enthusiastic about school, be nice to people – or have fun, basically."

I blew out a breath. That sounded pretty extreme, and certainly horrible. How was I ever going to find a replacement for Jagger when these were the sort of people I had to choose from? Jagger and me were just ourselves with each other, but it seemed like Other Chloe had to pretend to be someone she wasn't. That didn't sound like friendship to me. Friendship should be easy and fun, and that sounded hard and miserable.

"I dunno," Other Chloe continued, as she finished

tying her laces. "Sometimes I feel like I don't belong at all."

I knew how that felt, but it seemed strange that someone like Other Chloe would feel that too.

"Mum? I'm just heading out with the boys, OK?" Other Chloe shouted through to the back of the house. I felt a ripple of something warm in my stomach when she said that. "The boys". That sounded like I *did* belong, and I liked it.

Other Chloe's mum appeared, all serene, if slightly vacant in the eyes. She had perfect, neat hair, wore a floral apron, and had pearls around her neck. "OK, dear, but don't be late back – I'm doing chicken in aspic for dinner... Oh! Hello, Rocco!"

"BWARK!" Rocco replied, flapping his arms.

Other Chloe's mum stared at him, then blinked, once.

Rocco just stared back.

Not for the first time that day, I was beginning to think that all the stress was getting to Rocco and he was starting to lose the plot.

Other Chloe's mum turned to me, apparently not

even noticing I was in a wedding dress. "And, hi …
uh … Oscar."

"Otis."

"You were great in the Christmas show last year, I
remember you!"

"No, you're thinking of Ollie."

Other Chloe's mum smiled. "Am I? Oh well. He was
very good." She glanced out of her open front door.
"Why is there a donkey eating all my pansies?"

"Argh! We need to go!" Rocco replied. "Come on!"
And he shooed us all out of the door.

We trudged down the road, me with the
wheelbarrow, and Other Chloe leading the donkey,
with Rocco sitting on top of it, because he was *so done
with this mystery*" even though we'd only really been
investigating for under an hour. Getting the donkey
back to his rightful home seemed like the next best
plan, and after searching the internet, Rocco felt he'd
found the most likely place: "Monty Bonkey's Home
for Donkeys" – a mere 180 kilometres away, according
to Google Maps. Estimated arrival time on foot: three
days.

"Giddy up!" Rocco said, patting the donkey on his rump. "We shall travel until nightfall, then find a place to rest, continuing at dawn!"

"Um, Rocco?" I said, hurrying up alongside him with the wheelbarrow. "How likely do you really think it is that the donkey would have come from somewhere that's three days away?"

"Perfectly likely!" he said.

"It just seems odd, if the donkey only appeared last night—"

"Stop being negative!"

"I'm not being negative, I just think there's an outside chance we *may*, possibly, have the wrong place."

"Nonsense!" Rocco sniffed. And then he shouted, "HALT!" and pointed at a poster that was taped round a lamp post, advertising the local amateur theatre company's production of *War Horse*. We all stared at the poster, which appeared to have a very familiar *donkey* in the starring role...

"Well, well, well!" I said. "Looks like we have a star in our midst!"

Rocco rolled his eyes. "Ugh! I *told you* there was *no way* this donkey would have come from somewhere that's three days away. Thank goodness for my keen eyes and quick thinking!"

I stifled a smile. "Thank goodness, Rocco. OK, about turn, we've got our next lead! This A-lister must have come from the theatre!"

CHAPTER 12
SUGAR RUSH

Getting to the theatre involved walking through the market square and along the high street – hardly ideal when you're trying to lie low and avoid any trouble. It was mid-morning by this point, and it was getting busy, so I told Rocco and Chloe that if anyone should question us, we'd just claim that we were "actors, on our way to the theatre". This was only half a lie, since we *were* on our way to the theatre, and it was another great way of hiding in plain sight, just like we'd done at the bus stop. Plus, actors can get away with anything. Like, would you, if you were in charge of a school with hundreds of innocent children, let in three adults in white lab coats splattered with what looks like blood? No, you wouldn't. Unless they said they were actors putting on a play about recycling in the school hall, in which case the teachers would be all, "WELCOME, WEIRD ADULTS! PLEASE ENTERTAIN THESE KIDS WHILE WE GO BACK TO THE STAFF ROOM TO EAT CAKE!"

So this was all going fine, we were walking along, saying things like, "We're ac-*tors*!" and, "*Mmmm-yeeesss,* life on the boards! Break a leg! Call my agent!" – like, it all sounded totally legit – when the first bad thing happened.

Bad Thing 1

Chloe started sniffing me. And not just one little sniff, but really ... *snuffling*, you know? Like a sort of pig. Everything was fine, totally normal (well, normal for us): Rocco was sitting on the donkey, Chloe was leading it, and we'd just passed a small crowd giving a busker a round of applause, when suddenly:

SNIFF! SNIFF! SNUFFLE!

... and Chloe had her nose right in my armpit.

"Um ... hi?" I said.

"You. Smell. *Divine!*" she purred.

"Do I? Um ... thanks?"

I thought that would be it, but no. The sniffing carried on. "Mmmmm!" she said. "What *is* that smell?"

"*That,*" I said confidently, "is the delightful scent of *Elderly Spices!*" Good old Jagger. He knows all the impressive body sprays and aftershaves.

"Are you *sure* that's what it's called?" Rocco said.

"Pretty sure, yes," I replied.

Chloe took a deep lungful of my delightful aroma. "Who cares what it's called? I could smell you *all day long!*"

That was great, but (a) this was getting a bit weird now, and (b) we really had quite a lot of stuff to do. Meanwhile, distracted by how *great* I smelled, Chloe had dropped the donkey's rope, and this directly led to...

Bad Thing 2

"WAAAAAAH!" Rocco screamed, as the donkey, probably craving a new sugar hit after polishing off the chocolate fountain earlier, and taking advantage of his sudden freedom, made a bolt for a cake stand in the market, with Rocco still clinging on to his back. "HELP!"

"Oh, no!" I squealed, running after Rocco and the donkey, as Chloe ran after me, sniffing and shouting, "Let me smell you, you heavenly-scented creature!"

The donkey had his massive snout stuffed into a pile of brownies. "Get him off! Off!" shouted the stall owner, who was a fierce-looking woman with a red face and no neck, in an apron. "What do you think you're doing, you FERAL, IDIOTIC *CHILDREN?!*"

I tried to grab the donkey's lead, but, possibly sensing I was coming to spoil his fun, he flicked his head in the other direction, and started to chow down on a massive chocolate gateau, while I flailed around on the floor, all twisted up in my wedding dress, trying to grab the dancing rope.

I felt a nose in my trainer, and glanced behind me to see Chloe sniffing my feet. "Otis! Such sweet, sweet-scented tootsies!" she said.

By this point, having lost her entire stock of brownies, a chocolate gateau, and with the donkey now making a beeline for a banoffee pie, the stall owner took matters into her own hands and started shooing the donkey away, waving a big spatula about, and shouting:

"OUT! GET OUT OF IT! YOU *MONSTER!*"

Which was a bit harsh, I thought.

"I'm sorry!" Rocco bleated, looking back at the stall owner, and clinging on for dear life as the donkey

jumped back, clearly alarmed at all the horrible shouting. "My dad will pay for the damage! Call him! He'll put it on his—" The donkey bucked. "Aaaaaaaaaamex!"

The donkey was clearly scared, and I know that because what happened next was...

Bad Thing 3

Sometimes, when people are scared, they have little "accidents", don't they? Turns out, donkeys do too, because it was at this moment, terrified by the angry stall owner shouting and waving, that the donkey bucked about, kicked over the entire cake stall, sending everything flying, then opened his bowels and unleashed a torrent of donkey poop all over the ground by the stall. Indeed, such was the force of this poop explosion, it sprayed on to the rest of the cakes that the donkey hadn't yet eaten. I mean, sure, it was pretty horrific.

"I think he might have the runs because he's eaten a lot of bad stuff today," I tried to explain to the stall owner. "I mean, donkeys shouldn't really eat chocolate and cakes..." Or, indeed, any of the leftovers from Rocco's party.

The woman looked back at me in utter disbelief.

"It's OK, because we're actors?" Rocco offered, by way of explanation.

As the stall owner started scrambling around for all her takings that the donkey had sent flying,

Bad Thing 4

… happened.

"What *on earth* is going on?"

It was Posh Chloe and Sporty Chloe, standing in front of us, arms crossed, looking totally appalled at the unfolding scene.

I looked at Rocco, who was staring, open-mouthed, at the Chloes. It seemed like he was frozen, unable to speak. Other Chloe, meanwhile, who was still on her knees sniffing my trainers, looked up and gave them a toothy grin. "Have you smelled this? It's amazing!"

"Right!" Posh Chloe said. "First of all, (a) *you*, Chloe, have seriously overstepped the mark this time. Wearing dungarees and sniffing feet while surrounded by donkey poo is *not* how the Chloes behave, and you are now banished from our group. *Banished.* And (b) Rocco? We are so disappointed to see you hanging around with these" – she glanced from Other Chloe to the donkey, to me, curling her lip slightly – "*creatures.*"

My eyes widened. *Creatures?* I didn't dare say anything though, because I would never win against the Chloes.

"And what is that terrible smell?" Posh Chloe continued.

"*That,*" I said, confidently, "is the heady scent of Mature Spices!"

Posh Chloe grimaced. "Really? Because it smells like *'Eau de Pre-teen Boy Who Hasn't Had a Shower This Morning'.*"

I shifted on the spot, looking down at my shoes. I didn't smell. Did I? Jagger had assured me I'd smell *pungent.* Many people had so far agreed that was the case!

"Rocco? *What* are you doing?" Posh Chloe said again.

"The marquee was a disaster zone!" Rocco bleated. "I have to get all this stuff back to where it belongs before my folks find out!"

Posh Chloe laughed. "Oh my god, Rocco Rococo is scared of upsetting his parents! I did not have you down as being such a … dork!"

"No! That's because ... I'm not!" Rocco said.

Posh Chloe sighed and flicked back her long hair. "Anyway, we'd love to stay, but Chloe and I have our performing arts class to get to, don't we, Chloe?"

"We do, Chloe," Sporty Chloe replied.

"You know, Rocco," Posh Chloe said, looking up at him on the donkey, "just because you've tried to hide your *loser* tattoo under that stupid hat doesn't make it any less true."

And off they went.

Rocco bowed his head and sighed.

"You OK?" I asked.

He nodded, but didn't look up. "Yeah. 'Course."

"For what it's worth, I think she's wrong," I told him. "It may say *loser*, but that doesn't mean you are one."

"Oh," he sighed again. "I think I probably am."

He looked genuinely heartbroken, and I wasn't sure what to do.

"You lot have RUINED my stall!" the owner woman declared, clutching fistfuls of notes and coins, as she stood back up again. "And I'll RUIN all of you too!"

I wasn't sure just how she planned to do that, and

I wasn't about to stick around to find out. I grabbed a cupcake, waved it under the sugar-crazed donkey's snout, then hurled it as far as I could down the street. The donkey charged after it, Rocco clinging on to his back, and me running after, enticing Chloe to come along too by shouting, "Smell me! Smell me!" because that seemed to be the only thing she was interested in right now.

"STOP THEM!" shouted the stall owner, running after us.

We darted through the crowds, swung a sneaky left up a side street, then a right down another, looped around, hid behind a hedge, then went back the way we came, taking all the backstreets and avoiding the crowds, the stall owner, and the potential for any more trouble.

By the time the theatre was in sight up ahead, Rocco seemed to have entered a terrible depression and even Other Chloe was dragging her feet. I figured it was to do with seeing Posh and Sporty Chloe, but I didn't get it. Rocco had never seemed to care what anyone thought before; he was always so above it all.

I needed to cheer them both up a bit. Like how Jagger would do with me, when I was feeling down.

"Come on!" I chirped. "Nearly there! And don't I smell good?" I grinned at Chloe. "Want another quick sniff to cheer you up?"

Chloe wrinkled her nose. "Ugh! Gross! Not being rude, Otis, but you smell pretty ... ripe."

"Ripe?" I said. "Ripe is good, right? Like a nice ripe fruit? A ripe strawberry? Everyone likes ripe stuff."

"More like a ripe *camembert*," Chloe replied.

"Cheese?" My eyes nearly popped out. "I smell cheesy? Why did you want to keep smelling me then?"

Chloe paused for a moment then laughed. "It was just a joke ... I dunno! Just ... mucking about! No offence. Really, no offence, but if it was between smelling you, and certain death, I would probably choose—"

I put my hand up. "It's OK. I get the picture."

We walked on in silence, leading the donkey around the back of the theatre, where a makeshift stable had been built in a cobbled courtyard area, with some bales of hay a feeding trough and water. The one thing the set-up was lacking was a donkey.

But not any more. Rocco jumped off, and Chloe led the donkey back into the stable, while I stood back, still confused about why Chloe had made a joke about wanting to smell me. Like, what's so funny about that anyway? It felt like Rocco and Chloe were both in on a gag that I wasn't part of...

It made me feel excluded.

Just like at school...

I froze as the ice-cold truth hit me: they were messing with my head! Chloe acting like I smelled good, but it just being a joke? The not remembering anything? All of this chaos? What if I was right all along? What if this was all some big trick? Some malicious fun to have at my expense? Rocco already told me he hadn't wanted to invite me to his party, but that my mum had forced an invitation. Mum was a stickler for the rules. She'd never do something that amounted to corruption. Rocco and his friends had engineered all this – including the little drama with the Chloes. It was all a hilarious, big con, and I was the victim!

"Know what?" I said. "I've had enough of this. And of all of you. Very funny. Well done. You nearly got me. Stupid me, I guess, for being so trusting. Well, the game's over now. *Goodbye.*"

"Wait!" Rocco shouted. "What do you mean? Where are you going? Come back!"

"I don't know why you hate me so much!" I shouted back. "What did I ever do to you?"

"Is this because Chloe said you smell?" Rocco asked. He reached into his little Hugo Boss man bag and pulled out a small bottle, which he tossed to me.

"What's this?" I asked.

"Peach body mist," Rocco muttered. "Spritz yourself."

"I don't want to spritz myself!" I fumed, red-hot anger coursing round my veins. "Seriously, you can all do one! I've worked out your little scheme – I *know* you've tricked me. Just leave me alone." I couldn't stop the tears springing from my eyes, but I quickly wiped them away, hoping Rocco and Chloe wouldn't see. That's what they wanted, wasn't it? My tears? "So, what, you drugged me? *What was in the chocolate, Rocco?* You put me in this dress? You all ganged up and plotted this whole thing, set it up, tried to implicate Jagger, knowing I'd stick up for him and—"

I stopped talking because Rocco had stopped paying attention to me and was staring down at the ground.

"Footprints!" he said, pointing.

I glanced down too. "Sure, it's muddy and we've been walking about in it. Stop trying to change the subject! I get it now! I've worked it out, and—"

Rocco shook his head. "Some of these prints aren't fresh, but they *are* from the same shoes. Look," he said, "same distinctive pattern on the grips, same size – they're mine! *They must be from last night.*"

I sighed. Rocco wasn't interested in a word I had to say! Well, you know what? *Fine*! Because I didn't need to stick around!

But then I glanced down to where Rocco was pointing and my eyes widened. Some of those footprints were mine! That meant ... that meant I *was here* last night. It meant ... my whole theory about this being a con maybe wasn't correct after all? Or did they take my shoes ... and put prints here? Why would they do that? My mind was spinning too fast to make any sense of anything.

"And these are definitely mine," Chloe said, pointing to another set of prints.

Chloe and Rocco certainly seemed sincere, like they

genuinely were confused. Were they faking it? I mean, if they were, they should have been winning Oscars and BAFTAs left and right, they were so convincing. They both looked at me. "Otis?"

"Yeah." I shrugged. "Those prints are mine, but so what? You somehow planted them."

Chloe sighed. "Otis, I'm sorry I joked about wanting to smell you. I guess ... it was mean of me. I shouldn't have done it. I don't know why I did." She reached out to squeeze my arm, but I shrugged her away.

"Otis, we're not tricking you," Rocco added. "Why

would I do that? I don't even really know you."

"And I don't really know you!" I retorted.

"Right." Rocco nodded. "So, I guess we're just gonna have to trust each other?"

I chewed my lip. For the first time today, Rocco seemed to have said something that wasn't entirely stupid.

"OK," Rocco said. "So, if you've quite finished?"

I sighed. "Fine."

"Do you need a tissue to dry your eyes?"

"No, thank you," I said, even though I did.

"A Werther's Original to cheer you up?"

I couldn't resist that. "Yes, please," I muttered.

Rocco reached into his manbag and threw me a little candy with a scowl.

"So the three of us were all here last night," Rocco said, as I sucked on my candy. "But also…" He pointed to a fourth set of prints. *"Someone else* was as well."

We all stared at the fourth, much larger set of prints in the mud.

"Someone with very big feet," Chloe added.

I accidentally swallowed my candy whole with a gulp, because I had a bad feeling about the way this was heading.

"Who's got the biggest feet in the class?" Rocco said, narrowing his eyes at me.

I blew out a breath. "No idea." I shrugged. "How would I know that?"

Rocco gave me a sarcastic smile. "You *do* know that."

And the truth was, I *did* know, because we did a "team bonding" exercise at the start of year six, and we all had to arrange ourselves in different orders: tallest to shortest, alphabetically by first name, and by size of feet. So I knew exactly who had the biggest feet in the class. Everyone did.

"JAGGER!" Rocco snarled.

"Well, let's just take a moment to reflect on—"

"Enough!" Rocco told me. "If you've quite finished with your hysterics and trying to throw everyone off the scent by suggesting – *frankly unbelievably* – that I was somehow behind all this, I think we should get back to solving this little mystery! I knew all along Jagger would be involved in this somehow, and I've been proved right! Next stop: *Jagger's house!*"

CHAPTER 13

LITTLE GREEN MEN

"Rocco! Jeez!" I said. "You don't need to hammer so hard on the door. They've got a bell!" I pressed it, hearing the familiar *Oink! Oink!* sound that was the Jung family's comedy door chime.

A moment later, Jagger's mum opened the door. She stared at me in surprise for a moment, and then her face broke into a wide smile. "Otis! And don't you look lovely! I think it's great you're being *you* and being *so brave* by wearing that beautiful dress."

"Thank you so much, Mrs Jung," I sighed, not having the energy to correct her.

Jagger's mum glanced to my side. "Hello, Rocco!"

"BWARK!"

"Right, OK," Jagger's mum replied, unfazed. "Are you with Jagger?"

"Ha!" Rocco declared. "We're not with Jagger because *you're* with Jagger! Let us see him!"

Jagger's mum blinked at us. "No, he was at the sleepover last night, so he's with you."

My stomach twisted. Jagger wasn't at home. Jagger hadn't been home since he left for the party yesterday. He wasn't at home, and he wasn't with this us. Jagger ... was AWOL. MIA. AFK. *But why?*

"We know he's hiding!" Rocco continued. "We need to speak to him about some pretty serious stuff."

Jagger's mum looked back to me, a smile playing on her lips. Jagger had played loads of pranks on her in the past, and I could tell she thought this was another one. "What's going on, Otis?"

My hand shot straight into the air. "I NEED TO PEE!" I announced.

"Um, OK," Jagger's mum said. "Well,

come in, you know where the toilet is."

I stumbled through the front door, which was barely wide enough for my dress.

"Have a look for Jagger while you're in there!" Rocco shouted from outside.

I tripped up the stairs and squeezed myself and my dress into the bathroom. But when I got to the toilet, I realized I actually didn't need to pee at all. Not even a little bit. Which was … weird. Maybe it was just all the stress and panic, making my brain play tricks on me, just like it was doing with Rocco, and maybe Chloe. That was probably just as well, because I wasn't sure how I was going to get out of this huge dress if I *did* need to pee. It was very heavy, and very complicated. How did people who wore dresses all the time ever go to the loo? I couldn't work it out. It was all layers, and material and chaos.

On my way back downstairs, I pushed the door of Jagger's room open. "Jagger?" I whispered. "You there?"

No answer. I pushed the door open further, and tentatively walked in. His curtains were closed, and the room was in half-darkness. I glanced at his bed and smiled. There, under the duvet, was a Jagger-shaped mound. *What was he doing?* I pretended I hadn't seen and walked over. "Jagger, you here?" I said again, grinning to myself. "Huh," I continued, "I guess he's not…"

And I flopped straight down on top of Jagger.

And a terrifying clown sprang up from under the covers.

"AAAAAARGGGHHHHHHHH!" I screamed. "AAAAAAARRRGGGHH!"

After I screamed some more (which I won't detail here), I saw it wasn't a clown, or Jagger, but, in fact, a dummy dressed up as a clown, which Jagger had set up in his bed with a trigger switch and hydraulic piston system, probably designed to give his mum the scare of her life. That boy had too much time on his hands.

"Jagger, you idiot," I muttered, as my breathing returned to normal.

And then it got faster again.

Jagger really was missing. And that was a very serious thing. I needed to alert his mum and maybe get the police/army/MI5/CIA/KGB involved, I wasn't sure.

Jagger's mum gave me serious side-eye when I got

back outside. "I heard screaming," she said. "Another little prank you boys are getting up to, huh, Otis? What's going on?"

My hand shot up again. "I NEED TO PEE!"

"YOU'VE JUST BEEN!"

"I KNOW!" I squealed.

Jagger's mum laughed and started closing the door. "OK, very funny all of you. Tell Jagger he'd better be home in time for dinner."

"Jagger's missing, though!" I blurted out.

"Yes, yes," his mum said. "I get it. This is another one of his 'hilarious' practical jokes. Just like the silly clown he's rigged up under his duvet. Like it's not totally obvious, hello!"

"Huh," I said.

"And only a fool would fall for *this*!" she continued. "Ooh, ooh," she mocked, "my precious Jagger is gone, call the police!"

"Yes!" I agreed. "Call the police!"

"Except," she replied, "this is all part of an elaborate joke, and I'm not going to fall for it. Have fun, whatever you're up to." And she closed the door in our faces.

After this setback, we all just stood in Jagger's front garden and decided to take stock of the situation because we really didn't know what to do next. Other than the donkey, we had made zero progress, and none of us could remember anything about last night still.

Then it occurred to me: *we'd been abducted by aliens!* It all made sense! And it was exactly what Jagger had said when we were chatting at the party about the Chloes – *that they were really aliens!* Was he trying to warn me? In the dead of night, we had clearly been zoomed up to their alien ship, where they'd performed mind control experiments on us, and we were still under their influence and command. We were no longer ourselves, but probably being controlled by some extraterrestrial hive mind, doing the bidding of some evil force, intent on overthrowing the human race. And they still had Jagger imprisoned on the ship. That's where he was. And the whole world was in danger!

This was too big for us. We needed to contact the President of the United States immediately.

That, or one of the lunchtime supervisors from school, because they were also pretty good at resolving conflict. Either way, it was an A1 emergency.

I relayed all this to Rocco and Chloe.

Who didn't believe me.

Jagger yawned. "You're just saying all that to distract us from the facts staring us in the face: Jagger's done a runner because Jagger did all of this."

"Our footprints were at the stables too!" I cried.

"He took our shoes while we slept?" Rocco shrugged. "I don't know the depths he'll stoop to in order to fulfil his ridiculous plans!"

"OK, don't believe me, but why take the chance? We should make tinfoil hats to interfere with the alien radio signal controlling us. If there are no aliens, it won't matter. But if I'm right, it might just *save our lives!*"

Rocco and Chloe considered this and, just on the off-chance my theory was correct, agreed to the hats on the condition they were "made from premium, professional-food-service grade aluminium foil" (Rocco) and could be "accessorized with some flowers, or maybe glitter and/or fluorescent streamers" (Chloe, who was feeling a sense of freedom having now been expelled from the Chloes).

I agreed to both demands, mainly just to shut them both up, and Rocco knocked on Jagger's door again to ask for some tinfoil from his mum's kitchen.

Jagger's mum leaned weakly against the doorframe when she saw us and sighed. "Hello, Rocco," she said. "What now?"

"BWARK! BOCK, BOCK, BWARK!" Rocco replied, flapping his arms.

Jagger's mum shut the door again.

"Terrific," I said. "Well done, Rocco. Gold star for effort."

"I couldn't help it!"

"Exactly!" I said. "Because you're under the control of aliens! You've proved my point!" I slapped my forehead. "I'm working with idiots!"

Luckily, a new idea came to me at that moment, and one that would potentially clear Jagger's name. He wasn't here to defend himself, so it was up to me. "Jagger's not the only person in the class with big feet!" I said. "Remember? There's someone else!"

"I have tiny feet. All of the Chloes have: it's a condition of membership," Chloe said. "One of two hundred and thirty RIDICULOUS conditions."

"Yeah, I'm not talking about any of you lot."

"Well, then, who?" asked Chloe.

I decided it was best not to say – Rocco would only charge off and try to break their door down. "This way!" I said, hoping my hunch would prove to be right.

CHAPTER 14
NICE

"Hoo, boy!" Tiana said, putting her (second largest in the class) feet up on her bed, as we stood around in her *incredibly tidy* room. She was wearing baggy, ripped jeans and a baggy black hoodie (classic skater girl, and pretty cool), with her hair done in Afro puffs (I knew that because I'd overheard her telling one of her friends about it once). "That was *some* party, Rocco! I can't remember a thing about it! Man, what was in that chocolate fountain?"

So! I wasn't alone in finding that chocolate suspicious… I thought about the fact we'd all seriously pigged out on that fountain. Especially me. A vague memory flickered through my head…

"And *you*, Otis!" Tiana chuckled. "Twice I had to drag you away from it because you were going to jump in; the third time I was too late."

I looked down sheepishly as Chloe muttered, "Speaking of chocolate," and pulled a bag of sweets out of her pocket. She sat back on Tiana's desk chair and ripped them open, like she was at the cinema and really enjoying my humiliating story.

"Yep!" Tiana continued. "Pulled you out again; like a drowned rat you were, but drowned in chocolate... Chocolate everywhere! Chocolate hair, chocolate arms..."

"Chocolate Balls?" Chloe said, offering her bag.

Tiana took a handful. "You even had chocolate feet. What a mess!" She gave me a smirk, but a kind one, like she thought I was funny rather than an idiot. It took me by surprise.

"Sorry about that," I mumbled. More to the point, was the chocolate fountain somehow the cause of all this? Is this why adults were always warning us not to eat too much sugar? Because bad stuff *like this* happens?

"You may claim not to remember it," Rocco said to

Tiana, his anger level rising, "but you were definitely responsible for some of the stuff in the *wheelbarrow* currently outside your front door. Look!" He picked up one of her trainers. "The tread on these *Vans* exactly matches the extra set of prints we found at the stables!"

"Yeah, OK, chill out, Scooby-Doo!" Tiana said, rolling her eyes.

"I'm *not* Scooby-Doo," Rocco said. "If anything, I'm…"

"Daphne?" I suggested.

"The one with that nice cravat."

"Oh, yes, *Fred*. Hm, he does have a nice cravat," I agreed.

Tiana lazily grabbed another handful of Chocolate Balls. "So, what you got so far?"

"We worked out that the donkey came from the production of *War Horse* at the theatre," I said. "And we know the peeing cherub with the missing winkle came from Sally the witch's back garden. Jagger's also missing. Oh, and we also need to make some tinfoil hats, because we've possibly been abducted by aliens."

Tiana blew out a breath. "That sounds like a *lot* of

mess. But sure, of course I'll help."

Rocco squinted at her. "Will you? *Why?*"

"Because that's what people do," Tiana said, chuckling. "Nice people, anyway."

Rocco frowned while he tried to compute this information.

"Plus, Jagger's missing, and Otis can't be without his wingman!" she added.

"Huh," Rocco said. He took a deep breath like he was gearing up to say something big, then put his hand on my shoulder and squeezed. "We'll find him, dude."

I glanced at Rocco and managed to smile, and Rocco smiled back.

"Nice people help; I'm being nice," he explained.

I laughed. "I know you are, Rocco."

He nodded. "*Nice.*"

For a second, I saw a future in which me and Rocco were buddies, strolling down the corridors of secondary school together, totally having one another's backs. But I wiped that idea from my mind pretty fast; Rocco was only out for himself, we had nothing in common, and he saw me as a joke.

"OK," Tiana said, sliding off her bed and starting to pace around her room like one of those detectives on TV shows. "I reckon the best we can do is carry on working out where the rest of this stuff has come from. Maybe along the way we'll find Jagger, and um … work out this alien abduction thing, which can't really be a thing, that's just plain ridiculous."

"It's legit," I told her.

"What else is in your wheelbarrow?" Tiana asked.

"Suitcase of sausages, inflatable sausage, four fancy dress costumes, an empty wooden crate…"

"Oh yeah, the crate," Tiana said. "And all those birds that flew out."

"Doves, actually," I said. "White doves."

I watched as the cogs in Tiana's brain started to turn, and then she looked me up and down. "And you're in a wedding dress?"

I nodded.

Tiana's eyes suddenly widened. "Oh no. Oh *heck*! You're in a wedding dress! White doves get released at weddings, don't they? Who's the only person we know who's getting married today?"

Rocco and Chloe clearly knew the answer straight away, because they exchanged looks of alarm.

My brain turned the question over. Wedding ... wedding... "MISS PERCIVAL!" I squealed. "Lovely Miss Percival! Our teacher!"

Tiana nodded manically. "And it looks like we've just accidentally ruined the most important and special day of her life!"

I'm sure you can imagine our faces at this point, but in case you can't, it was something like this:

CHAPTER 15
PIGEONS

"Otis?" Rocco whispered. "Are you OK? You've gone very still and quiet."

I didn't open my eyes. "I'm trying to think," I whispered back. "I'm trying to think what Jagger would do in this situation."

"Huh," Rocco replied. "Surely it'd be better to think about what Jagger *wouldn't* do, and do that instead?"

I snapped my eyes open. "Don't disrespect Jagger. He's a genius at sorting out" – I looked at everyone's fearful faces – "epic disasters! OHHHHH, MYYYYYY GOOOOOODNEEEEESSS! WHAT ARE WE GOING TO DO? Miss Percival is going to actually, literally KILL US!"

"Well," Chloe said, "she might actually, literally kill *you*."

I blinked at her.

"You're the one wearing her wedding dress," she added.

"So?"

"So, you must have broken into her house to steal it!" Chloe said. "That's multiple crimes you've committed. Burglary, stealing a wedding dress, and ruining the most precious and magical day of our poor, underpaid teacher's life."

"We're all in this together," I reminded her.

Chloe arched an eyebrow. "You say that, but you're the only one round here wearing our teacher's wedding dress." She sucked in a breath and shook her head. "You're a very bad boy, Otis. You've done a lot of bad things."

"You can't pin the doves on me! If I'm going down, I'm taking all of you with me!"

Chloe gasped. "No! Miss Percival will deliberately ruin our SATs scores as revenge! How's that fair? All I've done is steal the cherub, apparently, and I'm not even sure that would stand up in a court of law! You're the one literally wearing the evidence!"

"Folks, chill!" Tiana said, cool as a cucumber. "Arguing and panicking isn't gonna help. This wedding fiasco must be connected to everything else. So, Otis: *what would Jagger do*?"

I thought about it for a moment. Jagger was a good guy. He liked a prank, but his heart was in the right place. He cared. "He would try to put things right," he said. "Like, maybe it's not too late to get the dress to the church in time for the wedding?"

Rocco held his hands out. "And the doves? They all flew off!"

"Get more?" Chloe suggested.

Rocco rolled his eyes. "Oh, sure, because I saw they had 'buy one get one free' down at Tesco!"

"That's amazing!" I said.

"That was A JOKE!" Rocco barked.

After more arguing about where we could get doves from, and my questions (which no one could answer!) including:

(a) How could I hand the dress back anyway, when it was smeared in chocolate?

(b) How could I hand the dress back when I only had my boxers on underneath?

(c) Why was there a dress at all if Miss Percival was meant to be going to her wedding as Bridezilla?

(d) Shouldn't we at least do something to prevent the alien radio waves interfering with our brains any more?

… we hit upon an idea.

And that's how we came to be chasing pigeons around Tiana's garden, wearing tinfoil hats, trying to catch them.

"Operation: Pigeons Can Look Like Doves If You Dust Them In Talc" began with the classic "run and pounce" technique:

When that failed, we progressed to the more sophisticated "ensnare pigeons with pincer movement" technique:

And finally, the one you must have seen on classic cartoon shows, where you lay a trail of seed all the way to a big net, ready to trap the bird when the tripwire is pulled.

Of course, with all the commotion, this was the moment Tiana's dad made an appearance. "What is going on?" he demanded.

I was still tangled up in the net with the others, but I managed to thrust my arm up. "I NEED TO PEE!" I shouted.

"Your finger is up my nose," Rocco muttered.

"Sorry," I said. "Also, don't worry, I don't actually need to pee. I just said it because I'm under the control of evil beings from another galaxy, no biggie."

"Oh, hi, Chloe," Tiana's dad said, approaching the net. "Hello, Rocco!"

"BWARK!"

"What is wrong with all of you?" Tiana hissed.

"Aliens!" I hissed back. "And the foil hats clearly don't work! The signal must be stronger than I'd bargained for."

By the time Tiana's dad had cut us all free from the net, the pigeons had clearly grown bored, and just hopped into the crate by themselves.

At last! I clapped my hands together in delight. "BINGO!"

Chloe's nose started snuffling around the back of my neck, sending shivers down my spine. "Oh, Otis! Your odour is utterly *bewitching!*"

Tiana's dad frowned. "Oh, is that *you*? What *is* that?"

"That," I said confidently, "is the delightful aroma of *Senior* Spices!"

"Old Spice!" Rocco hissed.

"Mixed with a hint of peach body mist – *ooh, fruity!* – and a smidge of donkey poop." I smiled at Tiana's dad, who just nodded and looked a bit sick.

"It's divine!" Chloe smiled, still sniffing at me.

"Ha! She likes it!" I said, trying to shrug off Chloe's behaviour like it was perfectly normal.

Once Tiana's dad was so weirded out by us all that he just walked back inside his house and locked the door behind him, we set about dusting the pigeons with talc. It worked a treat, and they were transformed from dull, grey things to a dusty white in no time. We put the lid back on the crate and placed it back in the wheelbarrow.

"To the church!" I said. "Let's put things right! We've got the wedding of the century to save!"

CHAPTER 16
"I DO!"

We darted along the streets, Tiana on her skateboard, Chloe pushing the wheelbarrow, and Rocco holding up the train of my wedding dress so I was able to run and not trip. The plan was simple: we get to the church in the nick of time, I return the wedding dress to a frantic and worried Miss Percival, who will be so relieved and happy she'll forget all about me stealing it and maybe even ask us to stay. While Miss Percival is married to her beau, we'll prepare the doves/pigeons, releasing them at the moment the loving couple emerge from the church. Then we'll all go to the reception party, where we will eat a massive chocolate cake. It was all going to be so beautiful and romantic.

There was one issue though.

If I gave the wedding dress back to Miss Percival, I would basically be in just my pants. And I didn't have any other clothes with me. I hadn't really thought the whole thing through, and I'm not sure an eleven-year-old boy in just his pants is top of any couple's wedding "must haves" list.

But then I had the best idea ever! I could wear one of the fancy dress costumes we had with us! At least temporarily, until we had to give them back too; it would give me time to find some other clothes. The cowboy one really appealed, for some reason.

"Look!" Tiana cried, as the church loomed into view. "There's the wedding party outside! We're not too late!"

There was no time for a costume change now. We pelted towards them, bursting into the churchyard, gasping for air, the veil flapping forwards over my face, when suddenly someone shouted, "She's here! Finally, Helen! Everyone's waiting – we thought you'd changed your mind!"

"Um…" I said.

"Quick, quick!" a female voice said. I couldn't see who it was because of the veil. How did anyone ever make it to the altar in these things?

"You look lovely, darling!" said a man's voice. "I'm the proudest father in the world. Although I think you may have sat in something unpleasant ... unless you're having your tummy troubles again, Helen?"

"OK, wait..." I said.

"No time!" someone else said, pushing me towards the door of the church.

I heard the church organ start playing "Here Comes the Bride".

"Hang on!" I babbled, as someone shoved a bunch of flowers in my hands.

Miss Percival's dad took my arm. "I thought the shoes would make you taller than this!" he joked. "Or did you ditch the high heels? Is that verruca playing up still?"

"Ha!" I said. "Well..."

"Come on, darling!" he said.

He started walking me down the aisle.

Through the veil, I could just make out rows of people in the pews, all looking at me and smiling. Some of them started weeping. Others said things like, "Oh! Isn't she beautiful!" And then, once I was past them and they could see my chocolate-stained behind: "Oh dear, that explains the delay. I suppose she must be nervous!"

This was all going horribly wrong.

Where was the real Miss Percival?!

Ahead of me stood the man I assumed to be Miss Percival's husband-to-be, along with the vicar.

I had to put a stop to this.

But I was going to be in *so* much trouble.

"OK, the thing is…"

"What's that, my little pincushion?" Miss Percival's dad said.

"I'm *not* Miss Percival!" There! I'd told him!

"Well, you are for about five more minutes, and then you'll be *Mrs Longbottom*."

Ugh? Really? That was going to be her surname? But it was no good trying to object, as he couldn't hear me over the sound of the booming church organ. I knew only too well the trauma of having a bottom-based surname, and why Miss Percival was going through with a wedding that would see her become Mrs Longbottom, I had no idea. Except, of course, she wasn't going through with it, because I was. *Oh god.*

We arrived at the altar.

I took a breath, because I needed to be brave and just tell everyone there had been a mistake.

Miss Percival's boyfriend turned to me and whispered. "I love you, Piggy."

Piggy?! I felt sick. What sort of awful nickname was that?!

"Dearly beloved, we gather here to unite these two

people in marriage..." the vicar began.

I shook my head, but no one seemed to notice, or care.

"Repeat after me: I, Mark Longbottom, take you, Helen Percival, to be my wife..."

It was all happening. My heart was pounding in my chest. My mouth was dry. I didn't want to get married! It was too quick. I wasn't ready! How did I know if I wanted to spend the rest of my life with Mark Longbottom? I still hadn't even seen him! For better or for worse? In sickness and in health?

The vicar turned to me, and before I knew it, I found myself repeating the vows too, because what else could I do? After this, when everyone had stopped gawking, then I'd have a chance to explain everything, and we'd probably all have a good laugh, and then things would be normal again.

"Till death do us part!" I chirped.

"You may kiss the bride!" said the vicar.

"WHAT?!" I squealed.

Now, this was where things rapidly got messy.

I felt the veil lifting from my face.

"AAAAAARGH!" a man, presumably Mark

Longbottom, screamed.

I blinked at him and gave my best, toothy grin. "Hi?" I said.

"WHO ARE YOU? WHERE'S HELEN? WHAT'S GOING ON?!"

I couldn't help it. My hand shot straight in the air, as I jumped about on the spot.

"Yes, child?" said the vicar.

I tried to stop myself, but it burst out. "I NEED TO PEE!" I shouted.

For a brief moment, everyone just stared at me in disbelief and disgust.

What else could I do? I scarpered for the exit. It was all too late now. Cries of, "STOP HIM!", "WHERE'S HELEN?!" and "APPREHEND THAT CHILD!" rang out from behind me, along with various shouts, screams, sobs and wails of dismay and distress.

I burst out of the main doors, back outside, an angry mob following me, at which point, Rocco, Tiana and Chloe released the doves-that-were-really-pigeons from the crate. Clearly pleased for their freedom, they immediately took flight, creating both a huge cloud of talc, which entirely engulfed the entrance and front of the church, and a substantial amount of pigeon poo, as they offloaded weight to aid their take-off. My pursuers immediately started choking and gasping for air, while simultaneously finding themselves in a shower of poo, and the reduced visibility caused several of them to collide or trip over one another's feet. As a pile of angry wedding-goers built up on the ground, and as others thought they'd been hit by someone else and started a fight, the rest of us made a beeline for the horse and carriage that was waiting on the road. There was no time to waste: we all piled in, along with the wheelbarrow. "Quick!" I shouted to the elderly driver, who was dressed in a top hat and red coat with gold buttons. "Get us out of here, NOW!"

"Yes, ma'am!" The driver flicked the reins, the horses neighed, and we sped off down the road, some tin cans on strings rattling behind us, and a sign on the back reading *Just married!*, leaving the furious, baying mob behind us, spluttering, shouting, screaming, wiping poo from their faces, and hurling insults and threats.

As "putting things right" went, it felt like we were pretty wide of the mark.

CHAPTER 17
I NEED TO PEE!

Five minutes later, and the angry mob had disappeared from sight. The horse and carriage slowed to a more gentle trot, as we all caught our breath. I was feeling pretty cross, to be honest. Rocco, Tiana and Chloe had just stood back at the church and let me be taken down the aisle and married off – and they hadn't done a thing to try and stop it!

"Well, thanks for all the help back there!" I said. "Some friends you lot are!" I glared at them all, and they looked back at me in silence. "Oh, of course, we're not friends, are we? Never will be."

"Sorry, Otis," Rocco said, finally. "It all happened so

fast. And there were loads of adults everywhere being very important, and we…" He sighed. "We messed up. I'm sorry. But…" He glanced at me. "Just so you know, I totally *would* be friends with you. If that was … on the cards?"

I didn't look at him, partly because even if I had heard him correctly, I wasn't sure whether he was just joking. "Well, actions speak louder than words, Rocco. Jagger wouldn't have left me to fend for myself, that's for sure! And your words are very sweet, but you've got millions of friends, and the only reason you're making out like I could be one of them is so I'll keep helping you sort all this out." I shook my head. "And, by the way, we're doing a *really great* job of that. If anything, we're making things worse, not better!" I sank down in my seat as the carriage bumped along, and put my head in my hands.

"Anyway," Tiana said, "I've been thinking. It's weird that none of us can remember anything from last night, and it's weird that we're all behaving in odd ways. Rocco's squawking, Chloe's sniffing, and Otis, you keep saying you need to pee, when apparently you don't…"

I didn't look up. "Yup."

"But something must have caused you all to be like this," Tiana said. "There must be something that links you all together – maybe something you ate…"

"The chocolate fountain," Rocco said. "We all ate that. Some of us more than others."

I knew he was talking about me, but I just ignored him.

"My parents are always warning me about eating too much sugar," Chloe said. "Do you think all this could be a sugar high?"

"But it's one o'clock in the afternoon!" I said, still not looking up. "The effects of all the sugar would have worn off by now!" I sighed again, as my stomach growled. "Which reminds me, I'm starving. Can't we get some food?"

"Do you know, I'm still full up?" Rocco replied.

"I *need* chicken nuggets," I said.

"Well, OK," Rocco replied. "We'll try to find something somewhere. We'll make a detour."

"Thanks."

"That's fine," Rocco said. "Anything for a *friend*."

I gave him the side-eye and he smiled at me. *That boy.*

We all sat in silence for a bit as we bounced along the road, before Tiana, who had been deep in thought for ages, started being weird. "Rocco?" she said.

"Yeah?"

"*Hello.*"

He narrowed his eyes at her, probably wondering what she was up to. "Um ... hello?"

Tiana nodded. "Rocco, hello," she said. "Hello, hello."

He stared at her.

"Hello, Rocco!" she continued.

"BWARK!"

"HELLO, ROCCO! HELLO, ROCCO!"

"BWARK! BOCK! BOCK! BWARK! BWARK!"

Poor Rocco was flapping his arms about and doing chicken legs, and it took me and Chloe to pull him down and keep him from launching himself out of the moving carriage.

"That's it! Don't you see?" Tiana said triumphantly. "Trigger words! Rocco only squawks when someone says those very specific words in that order! You can say "Hi, Rocco!" or "Rocco, hello!" and nothing will happen..."

We all looked at Rocco. He was, indeed, silent and normal.

"Go, on, try it," Tiana grinned.

Rocco frowned. "No, don't."

"It's science, it's fine," I replied. I cleared my throat. "OK, then. Hello, Rocco!"

"BWARK!"

"Oh, ho, ho! Bingo!" I laughed.

"Hello, Rocco!" Chloe shouted.

"BWARK!"

"Heeeellloooo, Roccooooooo!" Tiana added.

"BWAAAAAAAARK!"

"Hello, Rocco!" I said again.

"Please ... BWARK! ... stop!" he gasped.

"OK," I said, "but just once, we've gotta! Everyone? One, two, three..."

"HELLO, ROCCO!" we all chorused.

Well, that caused him to go completely *BWARK! BOCK! BOCK!* bonkers. And then ... he tried to lay an egg. Now, there's a big similarity between squatting down and trying to push an egg out, and, well ... I think you see where the danger lies here, and between the donkey and the pigeons, there'd been enough accidental pooping for one day, so I did my best to scare him out of the idea:

Rocco! Don't! No eggs, else I'll scramble, poach and fry 'em!

After Rocco had sat back down and we'd all caught our breath, I asked, "But what gives? What's happened to us then?"

Tiana explained that trigger words were something that hypnotists used to make their subjects do things on stage. When Rocco heard the phrase "Hello, Rocco!" he was basically programmed to squawk like a chicken, and it was likely that me and Chloe had trigger words too, which were causing our weird behaviour.

"Hang on, then," I said. "So were all of you on stage with the hypnotist last night too?"

"Yes!" Rocco said. "In fact, the last thing I remember clearly is when he called me up on stage!"

"Same!" Chloe added. "I can't remember anything

we did up there, or even who else was up there with me, but I remember walking towards the stage!"

This explained a lot. We weren't under the influence of sugar (take *that*, Mum – sugar's *fine*!), and we hadn't been abducted by aliens (bit of a shame, if I'm honest – could have meant fame and TV deals for us). Instead, we'd been hypnotized, and the stupid hypnotist guy, Enzo the Enchanter (who clearly should be called Enzo the *Incompetent*), had failed to change us back to normal at the end of the act! That certainly explained our weird behaviour … although it didn't really explain how or why we'd ended up with a tent full of random items, or where Jagger was… But hey, at least it solved part of the mystery!

"If we can work out all the trigger words, at least that means we won't be slowed down by clucking, peeing or sniffing," Tiana said.

"Hang on, what about you?" I asked. "Aren't you still hypnotized too?"

Tiana shrugged. "Don't reckon so. I've not done anything weird, have I?"

"*Yet*," Rocco muttered.

Tiana decided we'd try me first of all, and so everyone

started saying words and phrases to see if I'd respond by shooting my arm in the air and declaring I needed to pee.

"Hey, Otis?!" said Chloe.

"What's up?" said Tiana.

"Would you like some pickled ginger with your sushi?" said Rocco.

I rolled my eyes at him. "That's very specific. Also, nothing going on here, needing-to-pee-wise!"

I sat back in the carriage smugly.

"Goodbye, Otis!" Chloe said.

"See ya, Otis!" Tiana tried.

"How about a side of vegetable gyoza with your chicken katsu curry?" Rocco suggested. "What? I think that's a perfectly good question. Pffft! Your trigger phrase could be anything!" Rocco threw his hands in the air. "This is so wild, don't you think? Like, how did all this even happen, Otis? Huh? I've no idea what's going on!"

I shot my hand in the air. "I NEED TO PEE!"

"Yes!" Rocco said with a fist pump. "I win!" He laughed. "Otis? *What's going on?*"

"I NEED TO PEE!"

"Hahahaha!" said Rocco.

"I NEED TO PEE!"

"Hahahahaha!" Rocco carried on laughing. "This is too good!"

Tiana frowned. "Hang on—"

"I NEED TO PEE!" I insisted.

"You didn't say 'what's going on?' and he still said it!" Tiana said.

"I NEED TO PEE! That's because I NEED TO PEE!" I said again.

Rocco looked confused. "So, is the trigger when I laugh?"

"No, I NEED TO PEE!"

"Hahahaha?" Rocco ventured.

"I ACTUALLY LITERALLY NEED TO PEE!"

This was, admittedly, an unfortunate situation. Having spent all day in a "boy who cries wolf" scenario where I was claiming I needed to pee, but didn't, I now very much *did*, thanks to having to *talk about peeing* over and over again and being trapped in a carriage with no suspension, having my bladder jiggled about. This was the worst time to need to go, too, heading along a road, with no obvious toilets anywhere in sight. And I certainly didn't want to make matters any worse with Miss Percival, whose most magical day we had already ruined. I was already married to the man of her dreams and had caused a number of injuries among her wedding guests, and I was about to round it all off by unleashing my entire bladder all over her expensive wedding dress. The dress! Even if I could find a place to pee, I still couldn't work out how to remove the dress. Sure, maybe I could find a big bush, but I couldn't pee with the dress still on!

Or could I? Nah, let's be real; Mum always said my aim was bad at the best of times, let alone if I was also cocooned in ten tonnes of fabric and shaking from the fact I was (a) stressed, (b) coming down from a sugar high, (c) starving from having not eaten all day and (d) still under the effects of hypnosis. I would have more chance of success weeing through the eye of a needle!

"Let's get to the park! There are toilets there!" Rocco suggested.

"How far is that?" I squealed.

Rocco shrugged. "About three miles. Maybe four."

I felt sick. "That's not gonna ... work for ... me!" I gasped.

Then, of course, because she's a-mazing, Tiana came up with a great plan that could solve a number of problems all at once: we'd head to Miss Percival's house, where we could return the wedding dress, thereby enabling Miss Percival to get married and me to use her toilet.

"Great!" I croaked. "Where does she live, though?"

"I can't remember exactly…" Tiana began.

I groaned.

"But I saw her once unloading some shopping from her car on Addison Road, so I reckon she must live in one of those houses!"

"How far to Addison Road, Driver?" Rocco shouted to the guy at the front.

"Five minutes?" he shouted back.

Rocco turned to me. "Can you last five minutes?"

I took a deep breath. "As long as it's a really smooth journey, I reckon I can hold it. So, like, nice and quiet, nice and calm, so I can focus; otherwise it's game over, OK?"

Everyone nodded in agreement, and Rocco instructed the driver to head as quickly – but as smoothly and calmly – as possible to Addison Road, while I closed my eyes and did meditation-type breathing and tried not to pee myself.

Nice and calm.

Nice and calm.

I was doing fine.

And then something went SCREECH!

ROOOOOAAAAAAR!

Suddenly, three beefy guys on motorbikes were alongside our carriage, shouting, "STOP, THIEVES!" and "GIVE US BACK THE LOOT!" They were dressed all in black, with rather terrifying skulls on their T-shirts, and I think possibly some venomous snakes, and they all had long, straggly beards.

I tried to steady my breathing. "Calm, calm, calm..." I muttered.

"You've got the wrong people!" Rocco shouted. "We don't have any loot!"

"We'd know you lot anywhere!" one of the bikers snarled. "Especially *you* in that dress!"

"Ohhhh, nooooo!" I babbled. "What now?!"

"Stay calm!" Rocco told me.

"Uh-huh?" I said, through gritted teeth. "There are three scary biker dudes baying for our blood, had you noticed?"

"Funny, I hadn't noticed!" Rocco said, rolling his eyes. He turned back to the bikers. "Go away!" He told them. "I know *feng shui!*"

"You're not gonna give us the slip twice!" the biker guy said. "No one crosses the Heaven's Devils and gets away with it! You're for it now!" With that, the three of them revved their engines and surrounded the carriage with their huge, glinting motorbikes.

There are lots of situations in which it's awkward to really, really need a wee, but sitting in a wedding dress in a horse-drawn carriage, surrounded by an angry biker gang hell-bent on revenge pretty much tops the lot.

I groaned again, in quite a bit of bladder pain, but also wondering what on earth we had done now to make these guys want to, in the words of the one with the tattoo of a skull and crossbones on his face, "griddle us to medium-rare" because we were "evil little toe-rags" who "deserved a good thrashing!" All we were trying to do was return all the stuff we'd found in the marquee! So far, we'd managed to place the sum total of *one* donkey back with his rightful owner ... and collected several bucketloads of more chaos in the meantime.

"Driver!" Rocco shouted. "Can you shake them off?"

"Outrun a fleet of hundred-horsepower Harleys? Not a chance!" the driver replied.

My heart stopped in my throat.

"On the other hand," he continued, "we might have a shot at some evasive manoeuvres on less welcoming terrain. Especially if we cut through the centre of town... But the streets are cobbled, so..."

"Do it!" Rocco told him.

"It'll be bumpy!" the driver said. "Hardly the kind of ride you lovebirds would enjoy!"

"Do it!" Rocco repeated. He turned to me. "It'll be bumpy."

"Nggg! Gah! *I heard.*" I winced. "Oh, boy! Oh, boy, this is awful! I've never been this full of pee, not ever! I'm, like, ninety-eight per cent pee at this point."

"You've got this!" Rocco told me.

But as we swerved left, flew over a bump and

careered through some potholes, I really wasn't sure I had it...

"Later, suckers!" Rocco shouted at the biker guys.

"Rocco!" I groaned. "Don't anger them more!"

But it was too late. They were even angrier.

"GET THEM!" the main biker guy shouted.

And with a roar of engines, a whinny of horses, and the squeal of an eleven-year-old boy who was in TOTAL AGONY IN THE BLADDER DEPARTMENT, the chase was ON!

CHAPTER 18
POP!

The carriage flew down the main road, swaying alarmingly from side to side, the bikers hot on our tails. Up ahead were two bollards with signs that read: *No Motorized Vehicles*.

That was it! As long as we could get through the gap, the motorbike gang would have to stop ... or incur the wrath of the town's *very strict* traffic enforcement team (otherwise known as Mum), who wouldn't hesitate to fine them and maybe even impound their bikes.

The horses galloped onwards towards the bollards, the carriage bouncing up and down with every bump in the road, engines revving behind us, my bladder seconds from exploding.

"HOLD TIGHT!" the driver shouted as we hit the cobbles and our carriage was sent flying up in the air. For a moment, it was like we were suspended – gliding, almost – so smooth and calm, and then JOLT! We suddenly plunged down, my stomach lurching up to my throat and back down to my toes as we slammed on to the ground, clipping one of the bollards, which sent us crashing into the other one. The horses charged onwards, dragging us beyond the barrier and down the street, leaving the bikers angrily revving their engines by the *No Vehicles* sign.

We slowed up a bit, to more of a light trot.

We'd done it!

But all that bouncing and lurching around was too much. "We have to stop. NOW!" I squealed. "Get me out of this dress!"

Rocco reckoned we should pull the dress *down*, so I could step out of it.

Chloe insisted the dress should go *up*, and they pull it off me.

In the end, I'm not sure how exactly we did it, but I managed to wriggle out of the thing, leaving me in just my Mickey Mouse boxers, socks and trainers. The driver pulled the carriage over outside a shop called Punked (which seemed to sell lots of very spiky jewellery), but which was also, luckily, next to a large flower bed. This would be so simple. I'd hide behind the carriage and have a quick wee in the flower bed. No one would be able to see me – it'd take one minute, tops – and then we could all relax, get over to Miss Percival's, and save her wedding.

So, I scrambled down from the carriage, hid myself behind it, out of view of the rest of the street, and ... "*Ahhhhhhhhhhhhhhh...*" Oh boy, did that feel good, as I gave the flower bed the watering of a lifetime.

To be honest, I was really enjoying the wee. It was probably one of the best I've ever had. Until, that is, a series of terrible events occurred which sound totally made-up, but which are, sadly, the absolute, hideous truth.

I first became aware of it when Rocco suddenly started shouting, "No! No! Quick!" I glanced up, mid-wee, to see the giant inflatable sausage had somehow come free and was floating away. Rocco was jumping up, trying to grab hold of the string, but it kept slipping out of his hands.

"Get it! GET IT!" Rocco shouted at the others.

Chloe jumped up, leaped for the string, missed, and bashed into Tiana, who was leaping from the other direction. "OWWWW!" they howled.

"No, no, no!" Rocco shouted, as he tried to clamber up on the side of the carriage to reach the string. But it was no good, the sausage was floating up, up...

I would have helped, but I was still weeing at this point. Like I said before, I was ninety-eight per cent full of pee, so this was going to take some time.

As the sausage slowly floated up, I noticed that a small crowd of very serious-looking people holding clipboards had gathered the other side of the carriage, who appeared to be on a tour of the centre led by our town's mayor, Marjorie Poppleshank, who was dressed up in all her official robes, meaning this must be *very* important.

"We're extremely proud," the mayor was saying,

"that our humble town has won Best Kept Flower Beds for five years running now!"

Meanwhile, alerted by all the commotion, a man with a frankly extraordinary number of facial piercings who was inside the Punked shop poked his head out of one of the upper windows and collided with the inflatable sausage on its way up, accidentally spearing it on one the massive, rigid spikes of hair he had. Balloons and spikes are not a good combo, and the giant sausage went:

It was really loud. So loud, it scared the horses, who squealed and bolted forwards, pulling the carriage with them, revealing me, still peeing in the flower bed, just as the mayor said, "Our famous flower beds really are the pride and joy of our local residents!"

Everyone stopped and stared at me in horror.

And I couldn't stop weeing because I was right in the middle of the flow now.

So, instead, I took my own advice from earlier, about being obvious in order to get away with things, waved my free hand at the mayor and the dignitaries, and said, "In this town, when we like something, we wee on it. Like, um … dogs!"

This seemed perfectly logical in the moment, although I admit that in retrospect it might just have seemed that way, probably because I was still hypnotized.

The carriage was now under control, just a few metres away from me. I saw Rocco, who was watching all this, slap his forehead and groan.

The mayor looked pretty angry. "*What* is going on?"

"Oh no!" I heard Chloe mutter.

My hand shot up in the air.

"Yes?!" the mayor snapped.

"I NEED TO PEE!" I shouted.

"Well, I think that much is obvious!" the mayor replied. "I'll be in touch with the school about this *abhorrent behaviour*! Please, ladies and gentlemen, avert your eyes from this *foul child* and let me show you the tapestry that the Women's Institute made to celebrate the time we burned twenty witches at the stake."

The group walked off, by which time I had finally finished peeing. Rocco threw the cowboy outfit out of the carriage. "Put this on so you're decent!"

"How did you know that was my favourite?"

Rocco shrugged. "I didn't. I just … thought it suited you?"

Once I was in my cowboy waistcoat, chaps, scarf and hat, I clambered back into the carriage, and we assessed the ~~calamity~~ situation so far:

- Police looking for us for stealing cherub with the missing winkle
- Winkle still missing

- Returned the donkey – yay for us! – but not before destroying a cake stall – bad
- Ruined a wedding – very bad
- I am now married – congratulations?
- Hunted by scary biker gang for unknown reasons connected with "loot"
- Accidentally popped giant inflatable sausage
- Mayor angry – telling school about flower bed wee episode
- Jagger missing
- We're all still hypnotized (possibly not Tiana though)

CONCLUSION: We are all in SO MUCH trouble right now.

One thing was for sure, we *needed* Miss Percival, and it wasn't just so we could save her wedding. Miss Percival was brilliant. If she could make fronted adverbials make sense, she could definitely help us make sense of all *this*!

CHAPTER 19

BRIDEZILLA

The horse and carriage pulled up at the corner of Addison Road. We got ourselves and all our stuff out, ready to bid our trusty driver goodbye.

"Thanks for everything, kind sir," Rocco said to him. "Tell me, are we the strangest wedding party you've ever driven?"

The driver shrugged. "Marry who you want to marry, that's what I say! Who am I to judge? You're a funny little bunch of misfits, but I like you."

I glanced at Rocco and he smirked at me. I smiled

back. We *were* a funny bunch of misfits, although it was weird hearing Rocco and Chloe described in that way. But, you know what? It suited us.

As the horse and carriage pulled away, we were left with the prospect of checking about a hundred houses, any one of which might belong to Miss Percival. It was going to take a very long time if we had to knock on every single door.

"Split up on different sides of the street?" Rocco suggested.

I shook my head as a genius idea came to me. "There is one way we can definitely smoke her out," I said.

And it was the *perfect* plan. Guaranteed to work, because it was something no primary school teacher would ever be able to resist.

"FREE ARTS AND CRAFTS SUPPLIES!"

"GET YOUR PAPER, GLUE AND COLOURED PENCILS HERE!"

"WASHABLE PAINT! MODELLING CLAY! ONE HUNDRED SHEETS OF BRIGHTLY COLOURED A4 CARD!"

Sure enough, within moments of us all shouting

this stuff, I saw some curtains twitch at a window, and the flicker of a familiar face. "There! Number twenty-three!" I shouted.

We ran over to the house and hammered on her front door. "Let me do the talking," Chloe said. "As a former member of the Chloes, she'll respect me and we'll stand more chance of not getting in trouble."

This seemed like a good idea, especially since I had only caused more problems – maybe it was best to let someone else take the lead.

Eventually, the door creaked open and Miss Percival appeared. She had make-up all down her face and had very red eyes. Either she was suffering from hay fever in a very big way, or I'd say she'd been crying.

"Otis? Chloe? Tiana?" she said, squinting at us in confusion. "Oh, hello, Rocco."

"BWARK!" Rocco cleared his throat. "Sorry, miss."

Miss Percival frowned. "What's going on?"

"No!" Rocco shouted.

It was too late, my hand was already in the air. "I NEED TO PEE!"

"He doesn't," Chloe said.

"He literally just did a really long one," Tiana added.

Miss Percival looked panicked. "Do you need the toilet, Otis? We don't want any accidents!"

"No," I told her. "But thank you, I'm all right."

Miss Percival nodded. "Why are you dressed as a cowboy?"

"Reasons," I said.

She looked at what was bundled in my hands. "And is that ... my wedding dress?"

"Well, funny story..." I began, just as Chloe nudged me to shut up.

"May we come in?" Chloe asked her. "Things have happened."

We all went through to Miss Percival's lounge. I know she's a teacher and so usually pretty busy ~~devising annoying tests~~ with marking and stuff, but the lounge was an absolute *mess*. There were takeaway containers all over the floor, two whole (empty) tubs of ice cream, the curtains were drawn, and an old movie was paused on the TV – which looked very icky and lovey-dovey. Miss Percival is always going on at *us* about keeping our tables and drawers neat and tidy, so, to use a word from the vocabulary display, this makes her a *hypocrite*. However, I sensed now was not the time to mention any of that.

Chloe launched into an excellent explanation of what had happened, and how none of it was our fault. "And so," Chloe said, wrapping things up, "the most important thing is that we have found your wedding dress, we've brought it back – Otis hasn't weed in it or anything, and that's definitely only chocolate smeared all over the back – so you can still get married as long as your boyfriend divorces Otis first."

Miss Percival burst into tears.

"Oh, don't worry!" I interjected. "I'm sure it'll be easy for me to get divorced from him. It was pretty easy for my parents. Mum just told the judge that Dad had run off with an air hostess, so maybe I can say that about your boyfriend, and then he'll be free to marry you and you will still get to be Mrs Longbottom, for better or worse."

Miss Percival continued blubbing. She seemed very

upset about all this. We really had ruined her special day. Maybe her whole life, the way she was sobbing and wailing.

I tried to cheer her up by saying nice things. "It's a lovely dress, though!" I beamed. "You'll look great in it, I'm sure. Although, I am confused because I heard it was fancy dress?"

Miss Percival sniffed and blinked at me with wet eyes.

"You were going as Bridezilla?" I clarified. "I heard Mum say so. So cool! A prehistoric sea beast!" I chuckled.

Everyone was silent.

"Imagine the vows! 'Do you take this sea beast to be your wife?' 'ROOOOOAAAARR!'" I laughed again.

Still, no one else was laughing.

Rocco cleared his throat. "Otis!" he hissed. *"Shut. Up."*

Miss Percival took a deep, sad breath. And then she patiently explained that "Bridezilla" does not mean she planned to go to the wedding as Godzilla in a wedding dress, but that it was actually a nasty term, used to describe a bride-to-be who is being really demanding and horrible to everyone about her wedding.

My mouth dropped open. "Oops. I'm, um… Maybe I

didn't hear right, then? I'm, um … very, very, very sorry."

I chewed my lip. Now Miss Percival was going to hate me more than ever. I'd stolen her wedding dress, married her boyfriend, and now I'd insulted her. I reckoned I could kiss goodbye to any privileges over our final half term – a shame, because I had my heart set on taking home the class guinea pig over one of the weekends, but at best, I'd be lumbered with the stick insect now.

Miss Percival sighed. "Oh, don't worry, Otis. Your mum's right anyway. I *have* been difficult. But that's because … I don't want to marry Mark Longbottom!"

We all gasped.

This was like a soap opera!

"Because of his surname," I said, nodding knowingly. "I don't blame you, I get *so much* grief for having a 'bum' in my name."

Miss Percival shook her head. "No, Otis. It's because he doesn't make me happy. You should never waste time being with people who don't make you happy. Life should be about *joy*. And you should spend time with people who bring you joy."

That made sense to me. Why would anyone want

to hang out with someone who made them sad? That's why me and Jagger were such good mates – we made each other happy. It was as simple as that. My stomach flipped. I wanted to find him. He was my joy, and I wanted him back. And then it flipped again: he would soon be leaving. Where would my joy be then?

I glanced at Tiana, who was nodding in agreement, then at Chloe, who looked kind of sad, and finally at Rocco, who had his head bowed, staring down at Miss Percival's carpet.

"I went out last night," Miss Percival continued. "I needed to get some air and think about things. I realized I couldn't go through with the wedding today. So I dumped the wedding dress in a bin in the park. After all, you can't get married without a dress, right? I came back here, locked the doors and drew the curtains, and I've been hiding ever since. They'll probably all show up here very soon, demanding answers." She sighed. "Anyway, it doesn't matter really. I guess I'm destined to be alone for ever. And maybe that's for the best."

Poor Miss Percival. She seemed very sad.

But also, it appeared I didn't steal the dress after all!

I must have found it in the bin in the park and taken it! But what I didn't know is *why* I would do such a thing?

Never mind. Returning the dress was the most progress we'd made in ages. We just needed to get the rest of the stuff back to wherever it belonged, and hopefully doing that would lead us to Jagger.

We showed Miss Percival the contents of the wheelbarrow: the cherub, the sad and deflated former giant sausage, the suitcase full of sausages, and the rest of the weird costumes. Miss Percival inspected the lot, and then gasped. "Oh, my goodness!" she said, picking one of the sausages out of the suitcase. "Do you have any idea what these are?"

"Yes!" I said, putting up my hand, like in class. "They're sausages! They are meat, usually minced pork, encased in a cylindrical skin and typically sold raw to be grilled or fried before eating."

Miss Percival looked at each of us with wide eyes. "Sausages, yes, but these aren't just any sausages. They're technically *saucisson!*"

"Oh, we eat *saucisson* when we visit our villa in the South of France," Rocco said. "It's a cured sausage, isn't it? A type of charcuterie."

"That's right," Miss Percival said. "And these particular *saucisson* are made from a very rare breed of pig!" Then she added, "Making them worth about *forty pounds per sausage!*"

We all stared at the suitcase packed with sausages. At forty pounds each, and at least a hundred sausages in the case, that meant...

"FOUR MILLION POUNDS!" I squealed.

"Four *thousand* pounds," Tiana corrected.

OK, maybe I wasn't great at maths. But still! Four thousand pounds!

"You're telling us that suitcase has FOUR THOUSAND POUNDS' worth of sausages in it?" Chloe said. "Let's sell 'em!"

"Let's just ... remember that we took these from somewhere," Rocco said, bringing us back to reality. "And we need to take them back."

"How do you know so much about sausages?" I asked Miss Percival.

"I'm a teacher." She smiled. "I know everything. And do you want to know something else? These sausages, plus the inflatable sausage you had, are highly likely to have come from the recreation ground."

"How come?" asked Rocco.

"The annual Sausage Fest is happening there this weekend."

Ohhh, so that all made sense. It would be a pretty big coincidence if all these sausages *hadn't* come from the Sausage Fest. Which meant, at some point last night, between stealing the donkey from the theatre and the cherub from Sally's garden, and taking the wedding dress from the bin in the park, we must have also turned up at the Sausage Fest – which meant that was where we needed to head next.

I clapped my hands together. "To the Sausage Fest!"

There was a familiar snuffling noise by my left ear. "Ohh, Otis! Your delicious, sweet scent!" Chloe sniffed around me. "Mmmmm!"

I batted her away. "Sorry about her," I told Miss Percival. "She's actually still hypnotized from Rocco's party last night. We all are. Oh, not that I'm *not* sweet-scented, it's just—"

"You're not," Rocco told me.

"How dare you?" I said. "I smell of Aged Spices!"

Rocco shook his head. "*Old* Spice! How many times?! Anyway, I know the trigger for Chloe now. It's when someone claps. That's when she starts sniffing you."

"Yuuuuum!" Chloe added, taking a deep lungful of air from under my armpit.

Miss Percival frowned. "Can one of you explain *what is going—*"

"Don't finish that sentence!" Rocco bleated. "If you do, Otis will say he needs to pee. And he doesn't. Do you?"

I shook my head.

"OK," Miss Percival said. "Would you all like a snack? You must be hungry. Then you can explain what is … happening here, and then take the sausages back to the Sausage Fest."

"I'm still not peckish," Rocco said. "Mm, although I could maybe manage a piece of sushi, if you have some?"

"I haven't."

"I'm gluten free," Chloe added.

"Can't have peanuts," Tiana said. "Or any vegetables

that are green or red."

"And too much dairy flares up my itchy … uh, my itchy … I sometimes get an itchy … well, it doesn't matter, because I have cream for it anyway," I said. "So hit me up with all the MIIIIILLLLK!"

In the end, Miss Percival decided to scrap her offer of a snack, so instead we told her all about the hypnosis while starving to death.

"Well, you've got to get it sorted!" she said, afterwards. "I can't have you all behaving like this in class on Monday!"

"One step ahead of you," Tiana said. "I've been trying to find that hypnotist dude on the internet. I think I found his website…"

"Yes! Well done, Tiana!" I punched the air. "*You da G.O.A.T.!*"

She seemed to wince slightly. "I'm really not, but thanks," she muttered. She blew out a breath. "Gotta say, Rocco, he charges pretty hefty fees. You'd think for that price, he could at least do his job properly."

Rocco shrugged. "You're only eleven once. Have you tried to contact him?"

"I've called the number, but there's no reply. I've just

sent a message via his contact form. Hopefully he'll get in touch, we can find him, and he can put us back to normal. Well, put you lot back to normal. I seem to be fine."

Rocco narrowed his eyes. "*So far,*" he muttered.

"Meanwhile, I'll do some more searching," Tiana said. "Maybe he has a social media account I can message him on too." She got back to her phone, swiping and tapping away as she worked.

"You mentioned class on Monday?" I said, as Miss Percival showed us out of her house. "Does that mean you're not going to the deadly volcano for your honeymoon?"

"That's right," Miss Percival said.

"Awesome! Because I'm not sure how much we can take of Mr Banerjee and his global disaster simulations." I gave Miss Percival a smile. "Also, we really miss you."

Miss Percival smiled back and ruffled my hair. "Miss you lot too."

"Who needs a husband when you've got fifteen boys in year six!" Rocco added. "We can do everything a husband would do – read you poetry, I can make cupcakes and Otis can probably mow the lawn..."

"As long as an adult holds the electric cable and supervises!" I beamed.

"See!" Rocco said. "Some would call you the luckiest woman alive!"

Rocco was right. Miss Percival was *so* lucky to have us all. And we were lucky to have her.

"And you're definitely not alone," he added. "We're a team, aren't we?" He glanced at us with a hopeful smile.

"We are," Miss Percival said. "So, go on, *team*. Go and finish sorting this mess out."

CHAPTER 20
SAUSAGES

You wouldn't think sausages would be so popular, would you? Don't get me wrong, I like a tasty sausage as much as the next guy, but this Sausage Fest was ridiculous. The recreation ground was absolutely rammed with sausage fans, streaming around all the various stalls and stands, which were all celebrating, selling or cooking sausages. Organic sausages, artisan sausages, sausages from every corner of the globe, sausage recipes by top sausage chefs, and even sideshows! Pin the sausage in the bun, hook a sausage, and a weird game of sausage darts. Meanwhile, you could also ride a sausage – a giant sausage-shaped thing you could sit in, which swung up high and back down again, while the occupants screamed in delight. Boy, these folk sure did love sausages.

It was pretty obvious where the inflatable sausage had come from. All around, similar balloons decorated the entire

recreation ground, flying high above the stalls and stands.

On the plus side, there were so many it probably meant no one would be bothered about the fact we'd nabbed – and popped – one, so we took a team decision to put it straight in one of the bins.

But that still left the suitcase with four thousand pounds' worth of rare sausage inside, which felt like a much bigger deal. We walked around for ages, checking out all the places selling sausages, but nowhere seemed to be selling anything nearly as expensive as what we had in the case.

Eventually, tired and hot, we flopped down on a spare patch of grass, just by the inflatable bouncy sausage. We all sighed, but Rocco let out the biggest sigh of all.

"What's up?" I asked. "Worried we'll never sort it all out?"

Rocco shook his head.

"What, then? I'm sure your parents will forgive you, and I'm sure Tiana will track down Enzo and he'll sort out the hypnosis thing..."

"Still on it!" Tiana said, looking up from her phone for a second.

"It'll all be OK, you'll—"

"It's not that!" Rocco interrupted. "It's not that at all. It's something Miss Percival said. About not spending time with people who don't make you happy. Well..." He stared down hard at the ground. "The thing is, the other two Chloes don't make me happy. I have to behave a certain way when I'm with them."

I frowned. "How do you mean?"

"Everything's always so serious with them, just like Chloe was saying earlier. We never joke about. We never enjoy ourselves."

Chloe nodded sadly.

He shrugged. "I know today's been stressful, but I've also had a lot of fun. With all of you." He swallowed. "I just feel like I've been able to be myself. It makes me feel really jealous of you, Otis."

My eyes widened. "What?! Are you joking?"

Rocco shook his head. "You and Jagger, you're so ... complete. You've got all the banter; all the jokes. I want to have a friend like that."

"I had no idea," I said. "I always assumed you'd never want to be friends with someone like me or Jagger.

You always seemed so distant and untouchable and god-like!"

"Because Posh and Sporty Chloe make me be like that! Like, that Lego you got me for my present…" Rocco continued.

"Yeah, sorry about that," I muttered. "I didn't realize that—"

"But I *love* Lego!' Rocco interrupted. "Except the Chloes think it's kids' stuff, so I had to act like I wasn't bothered about it. See? Always so serious!"

"If you don't like the Chloes, then maybe don't hang around with them?" Tiana suggested. "It's not like you don't have lots of friends! They were all at your party!"

Rocco laughed. "Oh, sure! All of my other amazing friends who ran off at the first hint of trouble this morning?" He took an unsteady breath. "The fact is, they were all falling over themselves to come to my party, but the minute I needed them, not one of them was there for me … just like my parents – no one really cares."

It was then I realized that Rocco was crying. He was trying to hold the sobs in, trying to make them really quiet, but they kept bubbling up out of him, his shoulders shaking as he tried to stay in control.

I glanced at the others.

Tiana nodded and cocked her head towards him.

So I shuffled up next to him and put my arm across his shoulders. "Jagger's not coming to secondary school with us. He got a place at performing arts school. I've been terrified that I'm just going to be alone, and I never thought I could end up with a brilliant friend like you, Rocco."

"Or us?" Tiana added, indicating herself and Chloe.

I looked at them in disbelief. They wanted to be mates too?

"Tiana, you're the G.O.A.T, right? You're brilliant!" I said. "Why would you want to hang out with me?"

"'Cause you're funny and you make me laugh, and you don't always talk about sport like the other people I know?" she replied. "Also, I'm really *not* the Greatest Of All Time. You don't see me at the county athletic championships. I haven't won a competitive race in months. You just see what you see at school."

"And this is the first time I've hung out with people and not been told what to wear or how to behave," Chloe added. "I can finally be me, not *Other* Chloe who's not quite good enough, but *Fun* Chloe, *Happy* Chloe, *Don't-care-if-I'm-a-total-dork* Chloe!"

"Huh," I said, thinking it over. It seemed I was wrong about … *everyone*. I'd never given anyone else a chance, that was the problem. I'd just assumed they wouldn't like me, and that we had nothing in common. I'd never even thought to look at things from their point of view. Me and Jagger were so "best buds of all time" that no one else could get close to us. But letting other people in wouldn't diminish what we had. In fact, it would only make life better … because I liked Rocco, Tiana and Chloe.

I squeezed Rocco's shoulders. "Mates, then?"

Rocco sniffed, and finally looked up, wiping his red and wet eyes with the palms of his hands. "I'll try to be better at banter," Rocco said. "I'll be more like Jagger!"

"You don't have to be," I told him. "You're pretty great just as you are."

"Thank you," Rocco said, sniffing again. Then he buried his face in my shoulder and I gave him a cuddle.

"Otis?" he said after a bit. "You *do* smell really nice."

"Aha!" I said confidently. "That would be the delightful aroma of *Geriatric Spices!*"

Rocco collapsed in giggles.

"I don't know what's funny," I muttered.

Chloe's mobile pinged.

"*Retired* Spices? *Decrepit* Spices? *Past It* Spices?" I continued.

Rocco was in hysterics. "Stop! Argh, my sides!"

"Um, folks…" Chloe said.

"*Octogenarian* Spices! *Prehistoric* Spices!"

"Stop, I'll pee!" Rocco gasped.

"Folks!' Chloe said again.

"*Addled, maggoty, festering* Spices!"

"FOLKS, YOU NEED TO SEE THIS!" Chloe shouted.

We all hunched over Chloe's phone as she pressed *play*. It was some video footage that Posh Chloe had sent her, (*What a bunch of DORKS!* the attached message read), taken last night at the party. My eyes widened, as I heard Rocco gasp. So *that's* where the fancy dress costumes came from! I was dressed up in the cowboy outfit, Rocco was the sailor, Tiana had the dungarees and hard hat on, and Chloe was the police officer. We were all doing this weird dance, where we'd make various letters using our arms and bodies, along to the words of the song that was playing … Y … M … C … A. We looked like idiots, but to be fair, the song *was* very catchy.

At the end of the song, Enzo had us all sit down again, our heads bowed, while the audience cheered and clapped, and he went along the line, whispering in each of our ears, after which our heads would snap up.

"This must have been towards the end," I said. "It looks like he's waking us up from the hypnosis – or trying to."

"At least this explains the costumes," Rocco said. "So! They belong to Enzo! I guess when we finally find him, we can return them. Although why did he leave them behind when they're part of his act?"

"Hmm," Tiana said.

"What?" I asked.

"Just thinking," she replied. "It's probably nothing." She tapped the screen to freeze the video. "Who's that?"

I squinted at the screen, trying to make out the figure of one of the football lads. "Oh, it's Jack," I said, remembering that I saw him pointing his phone at me when I first went up on stage. "No doubt trying to film me humiliating myself!"

Tiana nodded, and started tapping away at her phone.

Rocco grinned at me. "I *knew* the cowboy costume was yours! And it suits you!"

"And you look *great* as the sailor!" I replied.

Rocco did a salute. "Shiver me timbers!"

"That's pirates."

"Oh," Rocco said.

Suddenly, it was like the sun had disappeared behind a cloud, as a huge shadow fell across us. Actually ... *three* huge shadows. I slowly looked up. There, looming over us, looking like we were going to be their dinner, were ...

the Biker gang

CHAPTER 21

HERO

"Well, *hello, Rocco!*" the biggest biker guy with the longest beard and the meanest face sneered.

Rocco's eyes widened. I could tell he was trying to hold it in. But, of course, it was hopeless, and suppressing it only made it bigger and louder when it did come out. "BWAAAARRRKK!"

The big biker guy looked furious, and lunged for Rocco, but was held back by the biker with the snake on his T-shirt. "Don't do it, Mick!" he said. "He's not worth it!"

"They're just kids!" the smaller biker guy added. (I mean *relatively* smaller; he was still twice as big as any of us.)

The big biker nodded. "I like kids…." he said.

I breathed a sigh of relief.

"... I could eat one right now!" he continued, smacking his lips like we were fillet steak.

Luckily, Tiana stepped forwards. "What can we do for you guys?"

"We want the loot back! We know you took it!" the big biker said. "Nobody gets one over on the Heaven's Devils!" He lowered his voice to a horrible snarl. "Just hand 'em back and no one gets hurt."

"We haven't got any stupid loot!" Rocco said. "So why don't you get back on your little mopeds and—"

Tiana pushed Rocco back and stepped in front of him. "Sorry about him," she said, smiling sweetly. "He's an eleven-year-old boy and is therefore completely bananas. Gentlemen, sadly, the only things we have are this peeing cherub—"

"With a missing winkle!" I interjected.

"With a missing winkle," Tiana repeated. "And a suitcase full of four thousand pounds' worth of ... ohhhhh. It's the sausages, isn't it?"

The big biker bent down, right up close to Tiana's face and nodded.

"Ohhhh!" Rocco said, before narrowing his eyes. "Are you guys smuggling them, or something?" He gasped. "Are you criminals? Are you in a sausage smuggling ring? Are you moving them across borders? Oh my god! POLICE!"

For everyone's good, I grabbed Rocco tightly and clamped my hand over his mouth. "Shh, shhh…" I cooed.

"We're *really* angry," the big biker guy snarled. "We've wasted the whole day tracking you down. And now … you're mincemeat!"

"Wait!" Tiana said. "We can explain!" She opened and closed her mouth several times. "Actually, we can't."

"We've been hypnotized!" Chloe explained.

The smaller biker laughed. "And now you're going to be *pulver*ized!"

Rocco wriggled free from my grasp. "If our fate is worse than death, at least tell us what happened!" he said. "None of us can remember a thing about last night!"

The smaller biker turned to the big one and muttered, "To be fair, we've had a few nights like that."

The big biker nodded. "Very well. We'll tell you."

"Thank you," Rocco said.

"We'll start at the beginning."

"Much obliged," Rocco said.

"And *then* we'll pulverize you."

"Fantastic, we're so grateful," Rocco said. "Wait, what?"

We all sat down on the grass as the bikers began their story. Apparently, they bumped into us when we turned up at the Sausage Fest last night, and were just being friendly when they got chatting with us and eventually asked our names. When they then said "Hello" to Rocco, well ... you can guess what happened. They took Rocco's squawking as him being rude, as though he was calling them "chicken". No one likes to be called "chicken" – especially a mean biker gang with a reputation to uphold – so things got pretty tense, pretty quickly. To diffuse the situation, and probably wanting to avoid a riot, one of the stewards at the Sausage Fest suggested that Rocco and the big biker guy take their disagreement to the sausage-eating contest – and settle their score the old-fashioned way: by cramming their faces with processed pork. Eternal glory for the winner, while the loser would be forced to get the word *loser* tattooed on their forehead.

Rocco was aghast. "You mean … I lost the contest?"

The bikers nodded.

"Huh," he said. "I guess that also explains why I haven't been hungry all day – I'm full of sausage!"

"Not as full as me!" the big biker boasted. "Then, after celebrating the win, we noticed our prize, a very valuable case of *saucisson*, had gone – and so had all of you. We've been hunting you down ever since!"

There was no doubt we had to give the sausages back – they weren't ours anyway, even if the bikers did seem a bit dodgy. But since the bikers were clearly the competitive type, an idea occurred to me that might just help Rocco.

"How about a rematch?" I suggested, as Tiana handed over the case.

The big biker looked up from inspecting the sausages. "Meaning?"

"Meaning another sausage-eating contest. But this time, if we win, you agree to get the *loser* tattoo removed from Rocco's head," I said.

The big biker crossed his arms. "And if *we* win?"

"You'll get the satisfaction of knowing you won *twice*." I nodded at them, like that was definitely a good prize.

"No," the big biker said, a wicked smile spreading on his face. "If we win, which we will, the rest of you all get *loser* tattooed on your foreheads too."

Oh boy.

"It's OK," Rocco said, dropping his eyes to the ground. "I don't expect you to risk that for me."

It was then I realized something: despite everything we'd talked about earlier, he *still* thought there wasn't a single person in this world who would actually do something for him, and him alone, unless they were going to get something out of it themselves – like a party invite. And right at that moment, as I saw the sadness on his face, I made the decision to show Rocco that he wasn't alone. That he *could* rely on someone. And that person was me. It's true, the stakes were higher than I would have liked, but we had to give this a shot – for Rocco. He couldn't have *loser* written on his forehead for the rest of his life! And sometimes, you just have to risk it all – for a friend.

I fixed the big biker with a stare. "You're on!"

"Agreed!" Tiana said.

"Aw, amazing!" I smiled, sighing with relief. "Thanks for volunteering, you're totally much more likely to win!"

Tiana frowned. "Oh, *I'm* not doing it. I'm vegetarian."

"Since when?" I protested.

"Since you came up with this stupid idea."

I turned to Chloe. "Don't tell me: you're vegetarian too now?"

"No," Chloe said.

"Great!"

"I'm vegan."

"Great."

"And I'm still full of sausage!" Rocco said. "There's no way I could eat another one!"

I sighed. There was no way out of it. "*Fine*," I said. "I'll do it. I'll do it for *you*, Rocco."

"My hero!" Rocco beamed.

CHAPTER 22
OTIS VERSUS SAUSAGES

I was expecting the contest to be a casual affair – just us and a bowl of sausages.

I could not have been more wrong.

It turned out that competitive sausage eating was one of the main events at the Sausage Fest, and took place in a huge marquee at the centre of the recreation ground. There were several competitors before us, and actual judges, a big stop-clock, a high-score leader board, and crowds and crowds of spectators, many of whom were waving large foam sausages in the air.

After some guy called "Dan, Dan the Sausage Man"

had won against a woman called "The Pork Princess", it was time for us to take to the stage.

"You can do it!" Rocco whispered, as he squeezed my shoulder.

I gave him a confident smile, but the truth was, I wasn't so sure. I hadn't been expecting all this fuss. All these people. All this pressure! Suddenly, I didn't feel hungry at all. In fact, I felt sick. Worse, if I failed, we were all going to have *loser* branded on our heads – and I was pretty certain that wasn't going to make things any easier walking into secondary school in September.

Me and the big biker guy clambered up on the stage. I say "stage", but it was decked out more like a boxing ring. We sat down at tables at opposite sides facing each other. My mouth felt dry as I watched my opponent flex his arms for the crowd, and then prepare for battle by limbering up his tongue and mouth by making a series of funny faces, which I guessed were designed to warm up his eating muscles.

"In the red corner!" boomed the announcer, who was standing between us. "It's the five-time sausage-eating champion and yesterday's high-score leader,

Mick 'Bottomless Pit' Fandango!"

The crowd went wild. I got the impression they were supporters of Mick "Bottomless Pit" Fandango. Maybe it was the banners screaming *Go Mick!* and the fact that most of the spectators were wearing T-shirts that read, *Bottomless Pit Fan Club*. Great. I'd proposed a sausage-eating showdown with an actual sausage-eating champion who had a fan club. Go me.

"In the blue corner! An eleven-year-old boy with no previous professional sausage-eating experience, it's Otis Bumble!"

There was the sound of three pairs of hands clapping, followed, inevitably, by the sound of Chloe snorting and sniffing, and then shouting, "Oooo, Otis! What a delightful pong!" which, of course, made the crowd howl with laugher.

"Bring out the sausages!" boomed the announcer.

The crowd roared their approval as two people dressed in – you probably guessed it – sausage costumes appeared in the ring. On the plus side, they were carrying small cocktail sausages. On the minus side, there was a whole BUCKET of them, *each*.

How many sausages were they expecting us to eat? Because in my head, I was thinking I'd eat about five?

"Just to remind everyone," the announcer shouted down his microphone, "yesterday the Bottomless Pit ate an impressive *thirty* sausages in *one minute!*"

Oh, jeez! That was one sausage every two seconds!

"Good luck, kid!" one of the walking sausages told me, as he plopped down a heavy bucket of sloppy processed pork on my table.

"Rules!" the announcer said. "Each bucket contains one hundred tinned cocktail sausages in brine. On the bell, you may commence sausage-eating. You may stand or sit, but only sausages fully swallowed will be counted. Spitting out or vomiting a sausage means a two-sausage deduction off your final score. After sixty seconds, the bell will sound again. You may swallow anything left in your mouth before the sausages remaining in the buckets are counted and your final scores revealed. Sausage Fest are not responsible for any participants who die, no matter if it's choking, cardiac arrest or exploding during the contest."

I glanced at my friends at the front of the crowd. Rocco gave me a thumbs up. He seemed to think I could do this. I wished I shared his confidence.

"Contestants ready!"

I noticed Mick standing up behind his bucket, so I stood up too. Clearly, he knew the best techniques. I'd take his lead, and maybe surprise him with my younger (and therefore more nimble) mouth, throat and stomach.

"On your marks! Get set!"

The bell sounded, and we were off!

I watched Mick immediately plunge his hand in his bucket, grab a whole fistful of sausages and ram them into his mouth. He kept his eyes fixed on me, staring, as he chewed. Intimidation tactics! Two could play at that game! I plunged my hand in too, also grabbing a handful of the slippery, sliding sausages, and shoving them into my mouth, staring at Mick the whole time, and even managing to give him a smug smile as I did so. But my smile didn't last long, as Mick then grabbed more sausages in his right hand, slapping them into his massive mouth, while scooping up even more with his left hand, and pushing them in straight after.

I needed to up my game.

I swallowed down my first mouthful, and tried grabbing sausages with one hand, jamming them in, and then more sausages with the other. But my mouth was full. There was nowhere for the extra sausages to go! I tried to chew more quickly, grinding my teeth, but the harder I worked, the less the sausages seemed to want to go down. I couldn't even swallow. Mick, meanwhile, was now packing another handful of sausages into *his* mouth, wedging in a couple of extra ones after his first couple of chews.

"Mick the Pit! Mick the Pit!" the crowd chanted.

Swallow! I needed to swallow! But I couldn't! The more I thought about it, the more my throat seemed to close up. Nothing was going down! If anything, the way my stomach was already gurgling, something was going to come *up* instead.

That's when Mick started showboating, playing to the cheering crowd, tossing sausages in the air like a juggler and catching them between his teeth … one, two, three, four … I reckoned he managed about five sausages in three seconds – at this rate, he'd beat his high score!

I made a valiant attempt to cram some more sausages in, squeezing and stuffing them into my resisting mouth, until I must have looked like a hamster who was about to burst. In fact, my mouth was so full now I couldn't do anything. I couldn't fit any more in, I couldn't swallow, I couldn't even spit anything out. It was like my body had frozen due to sausage overload.

Panicked, and on the verge of tears, I glanced, helplessly, at Chloe, Tiana and Rocco. What was I doing? What a totally bonkers twenty-four hours this had been! Why, oh why hadn't me and Jagger just stuck to our original plan of a nice, relaxed night at my house? If we had, I would never have gone to Rocco's stupid birthday party with all his fabulous food, and games, and DJs, and sword swallowers and—

That was it! The sword swallower! I remembered us talking to him last night, asking him what his secret was. He told us: you just have to clear your mind, not think about it, relax, and then the swords just slip down! Could that technique work for me now?

I ignored the cheers from the crowd as Mick drove

another fistful of sausages into his mouth, chewing them confidently. I ignored everything. I shut my eyes, breathed, and tried to stay calm.

And then, finally, I swallowed. My mouth cleared of sausage.

"It's *showtime!*" I muttered.

Keeping really calm and relaxed, I scooped up more sausages, popped them in my mouth, kept my mind clear, didn't think about sausages at all, chewed and swallowed. Another handful was right behind it. Working with alternate hands, I scooped, chewed and swallowed, the sausages sliding down my throat like butter. I didn't look at Mick, but when Rocco and the gang started cheering, I knew I was doing well. I kept my focus on the bucket, getting faster now, as I hit a rhythm. I must have been doing at least two sausages per second! The crowd started cheering too, some of them chanting, "Otis! Otis!" as, out of the corner of my eye, I saw Mick frantically trying to cram two whole handfuls of sausages in his mouth, but failing as they turned to mush, his face covered in sausage sludge.

Mind clear.

Focused.

Relaxed.

Just gotta keep eating them sausages!

The bell sounded.

Swallow!

The crowd went berserk.

Swallow!

Everyone was cheering.

SWALLOW! I couldn't swallow! Somehow, the final sausage had got stuck in my throat! Oh no! Oh... I tried thumping my chest, but it was no good. I tried pointing to my throat, but no one was looking at me, they were all watching Mick, as he ran into the crowd, giving everyone high fives. No ... air. Couldn't ... was this it then? Was this the end? What a way to go! Otis Bumble – dead at eleven, from choking on a sausage! A tear escaped from my eye. There was so much I hadn't done. So much I hadn't seen. The Taj Mahal ... the Great Pyramids ... M&M's World, Leicester Square!

I clutched my throat, slowly sinking to my knees.

At which point people started pointing at me and shouting.

Too late now … too … late…

Rocco burst through the crowd, and leaped into the ring. He ran up to me … and screamed in my face.

"What are you doing?" the announcer asked.

"He's choking!" Rocco replied. "You have to give someone a shock to stop it happening!"

"That's hiccups!" the announcer replied.

Rocco looked helpless.

At least he tried.

If I came back as a ghost, I wouldn't haunt him.

Then, suddenly, Mick was at my side. *Come to gloat, huh?* Before I knew what was happening, he had picked me up and was holding me upside down by my ankles. I felt a hand smack my back, and a whole sausage flew out my mouth.

And cool crisp air flew back in.

Ahhhhhhhh.

I coughed and gasped, and gasped and coughed, but…

He put me back on my feet again.

I wasn't dead.

No way would I try sausage-eating ever again. Honestly, juggling flaming torches while blindfolded seems less risky.

But maybe the organizers would take pity on me? Maybe I'd be given bonus points?

"Spitting out a sausage – that's a two-sausage deduction!" the announcer declared.

Or maybe not.

I glanced down into my bucket. It looked just over half empty – with the two-sausage deduction, thanks to my stupid throat not swallowing properly, there seemed no way I'd done enough.

There was a terrible silence as the remaining sausages were counted, before the announcer quieted everyone down again.

"Sausage Lovers! That was quite a contest, and it was close! But we have a winner! So, in no particular order … the reigning champion, Mick 'Bottomless Pit' Fandango, you managed fifty-five sausages! A new personal best!"

The crowd went wild, while I blew out a sausagey breath. Fifty-five?! No way could I have beaten that.

"Otis Bumble – our newcomer, young upstart … AND ON SIXTY SAUSAGES EATEN, OUR WINNER!"

I stared in disbelief as the audience totally lost it.

"Our new SAUSAGE KING!" the announcer boomed, as one of the walking sausages put a crown of sausages on my head.

Rocco jumped back on the stage, leaping at me and giving me a huge hug, with Tiana and Chloe right behind him. Even Mick came over and shook my hand. Finally! After eleven very unremarkable years where I'd achieved pretty much nothing, but ruined pretty much *everything*, I had actually won something! I *was* someone.

I was … *the Sausage King.*

Otis Bumble
Sausage King

CHAPTER 23
THE BIG THING WE ALL MISSED!

They say pride comes before a fall, and I can tell you that is definitely the case, because pretty soon after my INCREDIBLE VICTORY I became stricken with some really quite icky issues in the stomach department. I was carted off to the first-aid tent, where I spent about half an hour burping, farting, feeling sick, *being* sick, and other gross things which I don't need to detail here, but which I'm sure you can imagine.

I soon bounced back, though, and on my way out of the first-aid tent I bumped into Rocco, who was on *his* way out of the tattoo tent – having now had the word *loser* removed from his forehead. His forehead still had an angry red welt across it, but surely that would fade over time?

"Was it painful?" I asked.

Rocco looked sheepish. "Ah, um… It turns out tattooing children is all kinds of illegal, so the tattoo just *looked* like a tattoo but was actually marker pen, and it kind of comes off with water, soap and … a bit of rubbing."

I squinted at him. "Didn't you try that already?"

"No, I did not try that already."

I shook my head. Surely that should have been the first thing he would have tried! "What are you like?!" I said.

Rocco laughed. "I know! What am I like?"

We were still laughing about what Rocco was like when we arrived back to where Tiana and Chloe were waiting on some sausage-shaped benches near the music tent, where a band called the Baloney Homies were currently playing. The music was pretty cool, but Tiana and Chloe weren't dancing. They weren't even listening. Instead, they were both hunched over Tiana's phone, looking worried.

Chloe looked up as we approached. "You've gotta see this, boys."

We crowded round the phone. It was playing more footage from when we were all hypnotized on stage at the party last night, and the bit we were looking at seemed to be towards the end of the show, because Enzo was telling the audience he was "lifting the hypnosis" and then would bend down and whisper magical words in our ears.

"This is the video that Jack took at the front of the stage – he just sent it through," Tiana explained. "It's closer, so the quality is better, and I've been able to run it through some audio enhancing software I downloaded, so the sound is even clearer now."

"OK, so what are we looking at?" Rocco asked.

"We're not *looking*," Tiana told him. "We're *listening*." She cranked up the volume. "You can hear exactly what Enzo is whispering in our ears…" She held the phone towards us so we could get our ears closer. It wasn't crystal clear, but you could definitely make out the words…

"When midnight strikes, steal valuable things! Bring them back here!"

Enzo repeated the same phrase in each of our ears, every time telling the audience that what he was really doing was removing the hypnosis.

"OK, so that's … weird?" I said.

Tiana nodded. "Really weird."

"He didn't de-hypnotize us at all," Rocco said. "In fact, he's the one that made us go out, find all the stuff, take it, and bring it back to the marquee?"

"Seems that way," Tiana said.

"He programmed us to steal things from around town we considered to be valuable," Chloe added. "The wedding dress, the donkey, the peeing cherub with the missing winkle, the case of sausages…"

I sighed. "But why? Why would he do that? It doesn't make any sense. What's going on? I need to pee." I cleared my throat. "Sorry, I don't."

"We know," Chloe said.

"Does he just like to mess with people?" Rocco asked. "Does he just like a prank? Like Jagger?"

I blew out a breath. This really didn't make sense. It felt like we were missing something. And talking of missing – *that's what poor Jagger still was!* Was all of this somehow linked?

"Hey, Sausage King!"

I looked up in the direction of the voice, and saw Mick with the other two bikers walking towards us.

"OK, we're off!" Mick said. "But just wanted to say – it was a pleasure being beaten by you! And, fair enough, we were really angry with you after what you did, but it was pretty quick thinking to take the case while we were all distracted with winning the contest last night! Lesson learned! We'll keep our wits about us in the future!" He nodded at us all. "Take it easy, yeah?"

And off they went.

It was then I noticed Tiana. She looked like she'd seen a ghost, and her mouth was hanging open. "You OK?" I asked.

"Distracted," she muttered.

"Huh?" I said. "Oh, you mean what Mick said? About how we took the case of sausages while they were distracted? Yeah! I guess that *was* pretty sharp of us—"

"*Distraction...*" she muttered again.

I glanced at Rocco who shrugged.

Tiana gasped. "Of course! How could we have missed

it! It's so obvious!" She started jabbing and swiping at her phone, muttering things like "I hope I'm wrong!" and "I knew! I knew it!" while we howled at her to tell us what on earth was going on, and what it was we were meant to have "missed"? She finally looked up, grinned and snapped her fingers. "Boom! This whole thing – *everything* – has been one big exercise in *distraction*!" she said. "It's smoke and mirrors, designed to hide the truth by making us look at something else."

We all glanced at one another. "What? I don't get it?" I said.

"You wake up after a great birthday party to find a load of things that don't belong to you," Tiana said. "And not just any things – important, valuable things. Things that could get you in trouble if someone found out you took them. So, what do you do? What would any upstanding, good person do?"

I shrugged. "You'd return it all! Which is exactly what we've done. You're just telling us what we already know!"

Tiana nodded. "And if you're out and about returning all this stuff, where are you *not*?"

"Where are we *not*?" Rocco frowned. "Well, I'll tell

you where I'm *not*! I'm *not* at home, relaxing after my big party!" He blew out a breath. "I'm bushed! I just wanted to chill out today!"

"You're not at home," Tiana repeated.

I was still confused. Tiana appeared to be just pointing out the obvious.

"I missed this before," Tiana continued, now back on her phone. "I didn't join the dots and make the connection. See?" She showed us her search results. "Over the last two years, there are loads of newspaper articles about burglaries in the area, and what's interesting is they all mention that the crimes took place the *day after* a kid's birthday party, when everyone was out. Now, they don't all say *why* they were out, but after all, if you're returning lots of weird stuff that potentially made you a thief, you *wouldn't* say, would you? You would just tell people you were clearing up the mess after the party. Something else: all these burglaries took place at nice houses, just like yours, Rocco. After all, you've got to be pretty rich to hire entertainers for your birthday, so it figures. And you've got loads of nice stuff at your house, Rocco—"

I nodded. "Vases, old paintings…" I swallowed as it hit me. "Hang on. You're saying Enzo programmed us to take stuff so everyone would be distracted returning it the next day, leaving him free to burgle Rocco's house, because Enzo is actually some sort of criminal mastermind?!"

Tiana nodded. "Bingo."

CHAPTER 24
YMCA

"Hang on!" Rocco said, screwing up his face. "How could Enzo be sure everyone would be out? Like parents? Most kids would try to hide the evidence, like we're doing, right? Sort it out themselves, so they don't get in trouble?"

"Except, he *did* ask for your parents to come up on stage last night," I said, remembering. "And he seemed quite annoyed when it turned out they weren't there."

Tiana nodded. "I think his original plan was to hypnotize your whole family, Rocco. But he ended up having to hypnotize us when that first plan failed."

"But that still doesn't guarantee my parents would be out of the house!" Rocco insisted.

"Except, they *are* out the house," I said. "Because your mum told me this morning that she'd totally forgotten she'd won a family day at a yoga retreat."

Rocco chewed his lip, then picked up his phone. "Let's get to the bottom of this," he said, dialling his mum and putting it on loudspeaker. "Mum? Where are you?"

"Rocco, darling!" came the reply. "What a terrible day! We turned up at the address of the yoga retreat, but it turned out to be a *yoghurt* factory, so maybe I misheard and we'd won a day at a *yoghurt* retreat, and obviously I'm dairy free, so I've no interest in that, so we're on our way back in the car now."

"But … how come you suddenly remembered about winning the prize anyway?"

"I've no idea, darling! This charming man came to the door this morning, asking about something, I can't remember, and then I went back inside and it suddenly hit me – we'd won a day at a yoga retreat! Two hundred miles away. A bit inconvenient, but you can't say no to something that's free!"

"Mum!" Rocco said. *"What did the charming man say to you exactly?"*

"Honestly dear, I can't remember. I think he was advertising a new opticians, or something, because the only thing I recall is him saying 'Look into my eyes!'"

We all looked at each other. *Enzo!*

Rocco was shaking. "How far away from home are you, Mum?"

"About two hours!"

"Mum, listen carefully—"

"I can't hear you!" came the reply.

"Mum, the guy who came to the door—"

"You're breaking up! Rocco? Rocco?"

"Mum, I think we're being burgled!"

The line went dead.

We were all frozen for a moment until Rocco's eyes widened, and he squealed, "My house!"

Of course, we had to get back there. And fast. Calling the police on the way! Anything to stop Enzo! Enzo … who we all thought was just a joke of a children's party entertainer, but who was actually the greatest criminal mastermind this town – no, this *country* – had ever seen! Wow, when you look a little deeper, no one is what they first seem, are they?

But just as we all turned and were about to bolt off, the band on the stage announced a new song, and what felt like a very familiar brass instrument intro started playing, and suddenly we couldn't help it ... Rocco grabbed the sailor outfit and put it on... Chloe donned the police officer uniform, I swapped my sausage crown for the cowboy hat, while Tiana dressed up in the hard hat and overalls...

"WHAT AM I DOING?!" Rocco squealed, as he donned the little blue neckerchief. "My house is literally being robbed and I'm doing *this*?!"

"ARGH!" Tiana shouted. "It's the hypnosis! My arms... I can't control my arms!"

"I *knew* you'd have been hypnotized too!" Rocco squealed.

"This is clearly the only thing though!" Tiana replied.

"*Maybe*," Rocco said.

Within moments, we were standing next to each other in a line: a sailor, a police officer, a cowboy and a labourer, making letters with our arms in time with the music: Y, M, C and A. Over and over again.

"What is this song?" I babbled, as I pointed my arms in the air to make an *A* shape again.

"It's super old," Chloe gasped. "But I know adults *love* dancing to it at weddings!"

Meanwhile, a crowd was gathering around us, apparently delighted by our impromptu show, many of them laughing and filming us, and saying things like, "How cute!" and "Aw! Sweet!" which was all well and good, but we had a crime to stop!

Of course, the crowd soon started clapping too, which set Chloe off, as she started sniffing at me, which amused the audience even more, as I flung my arms in the air for the Y shape, and Chloe immediately stuck her nose in my exposed armpit.

"Mmmm! You smell *pretty!*" Chloe said.

"*Historical* Spices," I replied.

The audience just laughed and cheered.

"How … huh … long does this … stupid song … go on for?!" Rocco gasped, completely breathless, as we all made a *C* shape.

"Three minutes and twenty-two seconds," Tiana huffed. "As long as it's the radio edit. I have this very fabulous uncle who *loves* this song; he plays it all the time."

"It is quite catchy," I said, forming an *A* shape above my head.

"Great song!" Rocco panted. "When your house isn't being burgled!"

It was beyond ridiculous. We were all dancing around, singing about some sort of hotel, because according to the lyrics it was "fun" to stay there. Maybe, if we ever got this sorted, and we were all still mates, we'd all ask our parents if we could go and stay there ourselves one day. How cool would that be? Me and

Rocco Rococo, living it up at the YMCA?!

I needed to focus.

A woman in the crowd looked around at all the people, blew out a breath, and said to her friend, "Wow, so many people! Everyone's packed in *like sardines!*"

That was when I remembered.

Sardines!

The last time I saw Jagger – he told me he was going off *to play Sardines!* Knowing Jagger, he would have found *the best* hiding place … probably so good he hadn't been found … and Jagger loves to win, so I bet he was still hiding…

In a house that was currently being burgled.

Jagger was in danger!

The music ended and the crowd cheered.

"We need to go!" I shouted. "AND FAST!"

CHAPTER 25
THINGS GET MESSY

The van parked on the street outside Rocco's house had *Antique Removals* painted on the side.

"Hiding in plain sight!" I said, reminding everyone of my earlier strategy. "I bet you that belongs to Enzo, so no one questions him loading all your stuff into it."

Rocco narrowed his eyes. "Not if we stop him first."

I gulped down my nerves because it looked like it was very much down to us: no one else was going to help. Rocco still couldn't reach his mum. Meanwhile, I'd tried *my* mum, but I already knew she was working this afternoon, so her phone went straight to voicemail too. Out of options, we had also tried the police, but they didn't seem to understand about the hypnosis, and I think they got confused by the donkey, the sausages and the cherub with the missing winkle, and then to make matters worse, I told them I would pass them on to Rocco, who could maybe explain better, and they must have said, "Hello, Rocco?" because next thing, he was squawking down the phone at them, and I think that was the final nail in the coffin really. I heard them shouting something about "crank calls" and they slammed the phone down.

So that just left us.

Four kids (five, if Jagger was in there!) versus Enzo the Master Criminal.

We stood staring at the house.

"Wait," I said, clocking the alarm box on the wall of the house. "Your house has a burglar alarm?"

Rocco nodded. "Sure. We always set it if we're out."

"So, why isn't it going off, then?"

Rocco looked sheepish. "I guess I forgot to arm it before we left this morning, and I was the last one in the house." He cleared his throat. "Anyway, let the games commence!" He cracked his knuckles. "*Ow!* Ah, that really hurt!"

Rocco led us down the gravel driveway, our shoes

sounding horribly loud as we crunched along. Rather than use the front door, we slid along the side of the house, backs against the wall, towards the rear entrance. Along the way, we saw a window that had been forced open, a crowbar abandoned on the ground below. My heart quickened. *Enzo was inside.*

Rather than attempt to open the really complicated-looking folding patio doors, Rocco lifted up a plant pot, took a key from underneath, and opened a smaller side door instead.

"Amazing security," I said, rolling my eyes.

"And yet Enzo didn't find it and use it to get in," Rocco said smugly. "Probably because the key is *hiding in plain sight* – it's too obvious."

Huh. He might have a point.

Rocco gently turned the key in the lock, and softly pushed the door open. "Tradesman's entrance," he explained. "Shoes off."

"Good idea!" I said. "We'll make less noise if we're just in our socks."

"Actually, I was thinking about the carpets," Rocco replied. "They're velvet pile, *from Harrods.*"

I mean, whatever, Rocco. We all tugged our trainers off. I noticed Rocco's socks were designer and immediately felt ashamed of my counterfeit *Toy Story* ones, complete with hole for my big toe to poke out.

We crept through something called the "butler's kitchen" (I mean, how rich was Rocco exactly?!) which led out into the main hallway that I recognized from when Coco showed me and Jagger in the night before. Only now, several of the huge paintings I had admired had been taken down from the walls and stacked up near a door on the left beside a big pile of stuff. Enzo must have still been hunting for loot, collecting it all here by the door, ready for moving to the van.

"He's even taking my presents! *The Lego!*" Rocco hissed, pointing at the pile. "The low life!"

CREAK!

We all froze, eyes flicking up to the ceiling, where the noise had come from.

"He's upstairs!" Rocco mouthed.

We held our breath in the pin-drop silence. I wondered if Jagger was doing the same, wherever he was. I wondered if he even knew what was going on.

Footsteps.

"He's walking towards the master bedroom with the en suite bathroom and walk-in wardrobe at the back," Rocco said, cocking his head towards the stairs. "Come on!"

I grabbed his arm. "What are we actually going to do? Like, what's the plan here?"

"Um ... stop him?!" Rocco replied. "What were *you* thinking? Offer him tea and biscuits? See if he wants to join a game of ping-pong?"

"OK, you remember we're just kids, don't you?" I said.

"Funnily enough, Mr *Toy Story* socks, I'm aware of that!" Rocco hissed back.

Rocco adjusted his sailor's hat to a jauntier angle and cocked his head towards the staircase. "There's a panic button at the top of the stairs. We just have to reach it, press it, and the whole house will go into lockdown and the police will be automatically called." He looked at me. "*That's* why I know we can stop him. Just so long as he doesn't spot us first."

"You have such a cool house," I said, copying Rocco by adjusting my cowboy hat to a jauntier angle as well.

Rocco looked at each of us in turn. "We up for this?"

We all nodded, and I swallowed. "Let's do it."

We padded round to the foot of the Rococo's grand, sweeping staircase, and then, lying as low as we could to the floor, we began slithering up the steps, slowly ... slowly... Rocco was at the front, I was right behind him, Tiana by my side, and Chloe was on my heels. Rocco's staircase was top quality, of course, so not a single step creaked. Unfortunately, it was also incredibly long, and seemed to go on for ever, as we climbed up ... up ... still keeping as low as we could to the actual steps, hoping Enzo, as he walked about upstairs, wouldn't spot us.

We finally reached the top, and Rocco nodded towards a small white box on the wall just across the huge landing. "That's the panic button," he said, and glanced around. The coast was clear. Rocco took a deep breath. "Easy," he muttered. "So, who's gonna go and press it?"

Funny, isn't it? If someone had asked me on Friday if I was up for some incredibly dangerous almost-certain-death mission, I'd not just have been back of the queue, I would have left the building. But something big had happened that weekend. I wasn't just Otis any more: I was Otis the Sausage King! I'd proved my worth by helping sort the whole big mess out!

And I'd found a squad. They were my squad, and they made me feel like I could take on the world. Because that's what good people do, you see? They make you feel like you can do the impossible.

"I'll do it," I said.

A wide smile spread across Rocco's face. "Really?"

I nodded and squeezed his hand. "Really." I took a deep breath. "Wish me luck!"

But as I launched myself up the final few steps and across the landing, I guess Rocco's mum or dad finally called him back because his REALLY LOUD ringtone ("Born This Way", Lady Gaga) – blared out at full volume, echoing around the whole house, accompanied by Rocco squealing, "No! HUSH! OH GOD! OH GOD! SORRY!"

The only way we could have given the game away any more would be if we had neon signs all over the house that read:

Nevertheless, I bolted forwards, lunging for the panic button, reaching out to press it ... as a strong arm suddenly grabbed me round the waist and pulled me back.

"Not so fast, little man!" a voice hissed in my ear, as I was lifted off the ground.

Enzo.

He still had that stupid bit of beard on the end of his long chin, but now, without his cloak and top hat, and dressed all in black, he looked seriously evil, rather than try-hard and stupid.

I kicked my feet about, but it was no good; Enzo had

me in his grip.

"Not so fast, big man who's also a really bad hypnotist and a massive crook!" I heard Rocco say. It was wordy, but brave.

I twisted round. Rocco, Tiana and Chloe were standing at the top of the stairs now, forming a formidable line ... of kids in fancy dress costumes. But still! Surely Enzo would be trembling in his boots!

Unfortunately, Enzo just laughed. "Well, well, well! If it isn't the suckers – sorry, I mean volunteers – from last night's show!"

"We know what you did!" Rocco said. "And we know what you're up to! But the game's up!"

Enzo looked surprise. "Is it?"

Rocco gave him a really cool smile. Kind of knowing and dangerous. Like we had this in hand. With Enzo still gripping hold of me, Rocco swaggered over to the panic alarm, grinned at Enzo, extended a finger, and pressed it.

We all waited.

Rocco pressed it again.

Nothing seemed to happen.

Rocco took an unsteady breath and jabbed at the panic button. "Why isn't it working?" he muttered. "What's the point of a panic button that just makes you panic more?!"

"It's deactivated," Enzo said, smiling maliciously at Rocco. "I wouldn't be much good at this if I didn't disable all the alarms, would I? I certainly wouldn't want to be interrupted while your family are on a wild goose chase to a non-existent yoga retreat and the rest of you lot were busy apologizing for stealing things all over town."

His audacity was breathtaking. Classic villain! Admitting all his plans to us because he was so confident he'd get away with it all.

Admittedly, it was currently looking like that would be the case.

"Unhand me, fiend!" I said, adopting a phrase I'd heard various damsels in distress say in films.

Enzo didn't unhand me.

SLAM! A bedroom door burst wide open across the landing and smacked against the wall.

"He said, UNHAND HIM!"

There, standing a few metres behind a startled Enzo, was my knight in shining armour … or, at least, my angel in silver shorts.

Jagger!

Enzo didn't even flinch. In fact, he rolled his eyes.

"You've been WARNED!" Jagger said. "Now things are gonna get MESSY!"

And, *hoo boy*, they certainly did!

CHAPTER 26
TERMINATOR

Jagger swung into action. "Thought you'd get one over on us, did ya?" He beamed. "Well, you didn't reckon on these!"

Jagger flung open another door, revealing an airing cupboard.

"Pillowcases and drying pants?" Enzo said, looking confused.

"*Why are there so many doors in your house?!*" Jagger hissed at Rocco.

Rocco shrugged. "We need them."

Jagger rolled his eyes and flung open the door *next* to the airing cupboard. "Aha! You didn't reckon on

THESE!" he said again, as a load of balloons that were left over from the party last night tumbled out.

Enzo laughed, and I didn't blame him. A bunch of stupid balloons wasn't going to stop anyone.

"Ha!" Jagger said, batting one at Enzo.

It's pretty hard to bat a balloon at someone. You can really smack it, but the force quickly dissipates, and it'll end up gently drifting instead. The balloon floated towards Enzo, and lightly bopped him on the nose.

"Oh dear, oh, *ow*, the pain, the pain, you really got me," Enzo said in a bored monotone.

Jagger wasn't giving up. He batted a second balloon – which tenderly brushed Enzo's cheek – and then he picked up a third, which admittedly looked a bit different, slightly deflated maybe, and hurled that one, and—

SMACK! SPLOSH!

It was a water bomb!

What happened next happened FAST.

As water exploded over Enzo's face, Rocco screamed, "You've got your outdoor shoes on, you FILTHY MONSTER! Water and dirt equals MUD on our

VELVET PILE CARPET FROM HARRODS!" He launched himself at Enzo, doing a sort of rugby tackle, but more glamorous and dainty, like a sort of ballerina playing rugby. Dripping in water, and thrown off-balance by Rocco, Enzo dropped me, just as Jagger shouted:

"RELEASE THE BALLS OF DOOM!"

At which point he opened another door, pulled out a huge sack, and poured out hundreds of balls from last night's ball pit all over the floor. The balls of doom cascaded all over the landing, bouncing around, several of them getting right under Enzo's feet as he lost his balance, causing his feet to slip out from under him, as he did a full-on somersault, before smacking down on top of more balls, the force blasting him forwards towards the top of the stairs, where he shot over the edge and proceeded to tumble and bump right down to the bottom.

"HUZZAH!" Jagger shouted. "After him!"

"So much mess!" Rocco squealed, as he fruitlessly tried to collect up some balls.

"Rocco! Come on!" I screamed, grabbing his hand and pulling him down the stairs.

Enzo was groaning, lying in a heap at the bottom of the stairs, where we all piled on top of him to stop him going anywhere.

"Now, we call the police!" Jagger declared.

"Not so fast!" Enzo gasped, locking eyes with Tiana. *"CODE RED!"*

I didn't know what that was meant to mean, but a cold shiver passed through me, because it sounded like *bad news*. Sure enough, Tiana suddenly got this weird look in her eyes: kind of cold and staring into the middle distance, like she wasn't really here any more. She extracted herself from the pile of bodies on top of Enzo, and then this started:

"Hello, Rocco!" she said.

"BWARK!" Rocco replied.

"What's going on?" Tiana continued.

"I NEED TO PEE!" I squealed, my hand shooting up in the air.

Tiana then clapped twice, and Chloe started sniffing me.

And then she repeated the whole sequence. "Hello, Rocco! What's going on?" *Clap, clap!*

We were locked into our hypnotic states! Going round and round in circles, as Tiana cycled through the same trigger phrases, over and over again. So this was how Tiana had been hypnotized! Enzo had used her to create an insurance policy! As Rocco went "BWARK!" and flapped about like a chicken, and as I jumped around on the spot, needing to "PEE!" and as Chloe only now cared about sniffing me, Enzo was able to wriggle out from our grasp, dust himself down, and limp off down the hall.

"Good effort, kids," he grinned. "Just not good enough."

"BWARK!"

"I NEED TO PEE!"

Jagger just stared at us all in horror. "What in the name of *Beyoncé* is going on?!" he said. "He's getting away!"

"BWARK! BOCK! BOCK! BWAAAAARK!"

Jagger looked into my eyes. "Ah man, you're all still hypnotized, aren't you?" He shook his head. "OK. I'm going after him!"

In the background, Tiana continued to run through

the list of triggers, over and over again, as Jagger ran down the hallway, towards Enzo.

I looked, helplessly, at Rocco. "We need to shut – I NEED TO PEE! – Tiana up, it's the only way to break this – I NEED TO PEE! – cycle, to stop her talking!"

Rocco looked doubtfully at Tiana, who was now chanting the trigger phrases with determination, stamping her socked feet on the carpet with each word. He gulped. I knew what he was thinking. Tiana was bigger than him – most of the girls were bigger than us boys – and since she wasn't going to respond to gentle persuasion, he was probably going to have to gag her – and that was going to be tricky, since he was still squawking every twenty seconds, and she was likely to end up decking him if he went anywhere near her.

This was looking hopeless: Enzo was down the hallway, loading all of Rocco's prized possessions out of the window, while effortlessly keeping a kicking and flailing Jagger at arm's length, and there was nothing we could do to stop him.

Then my eyes settled on the Lego set.

Lego is great for lots of things, but it's really great for

one thing *in particular.*

Tiana was still chanting and pounding her feet on the floor.

"Rocco!" I hissed. "I NEED TO PEE! The Lego! Open it and—" I cocked my head towards Tiana.

Rocco's eyes lit up. He got it. He knew exactly what I was thinking.

"BWARK!" he said, darting over to the pile of presents, and ripping open the box of Lego, tearing open the plastic bag within, and hurling hundreds of Lego bricks all over the floor around Tiana.

It worked like a dream. Within seconds, Tiana had stamped her socked foot firmly down on a Lego brick, her face contorting as the searing agony that only comes from a foot on a Lego brick shot through her. "AAAARRRGGGHHH!" she screamed.

Rocco didn't hesitate, using the brief moment when she was distracted to slap a piece of Sellotape from the Lego box wrapping over her mouth. "Hush now!" he told her. "Hush-a-bye baby, sleep now!"

"Mmmmm! Mmmm!" Tiana replied, still rubbing and trying to soothe her foot.

I took a deep breath as we all fell silent. "Oh, thank goodness!"

"He's gone out the window!" Jagger said, running back up to us. "Let's get him!"

Chloe extracted herself from my armpit. "We can't! If we go after him, he'll just shout the trigger words at us, and we'll be rendered powerless again!"

"We need to keep a safe distance from him," Rocco said. "We're safe in here … the hardwood timber windows are triple-glazed … but he's outside, so…" Rocco's eyes settled on his pile of presents again, which Enzo had left in his rush to get out with as many of the Rococo's antiques as he could lay his hands on. A smile spread across his face. "The drones! All the football lads got me drones as presents!"

The five of us ripped the packaging off the drones, whacked in batteries, and prepared the remote controllers. "The box says age fourteen plus!" Chloe said, panicking.

"Don't worry, we've got this!" Jagger replied, as he opened the front door, placed the drones outside, then slammed it shut again. We ran to the windows of the lounge as we powered them up.

The drones rose into the air, just as Enzo was struggling down the gravel driveway carrying a huge oil painting.

"Aim for his head!" Jagger told us, as we manipulated the controllers.

I waggled the little levers around, watching as my drone shot up, plummeted down, and zig-zagged through the air like a drunken wasp. I had no idea how to operate the thing, so it was entirely luck, rather than skill, when I scored a direct hit on the side of Enzo's face.

"Bullseye!" Rocco shouted. "Ten points to Otis!"

I laughed as Enzo tried swatting the drone away with one hand, while trying not to drop the painting with the other. But then Tiana flew hers straight into his nose, while Rocco managed a direct hit up his bottom, causing Enzo to drop the painting and start lurching around the driveway, trying to duck away from the drones, like when there's an uninvited stinging insect at a barbecue.

I was getting better now, managing to zip the drone past Enzo's face several times as he spun around, just as Chloe aimed hers at the back of his head, crashing it into him, the blades getting entangled in his hair.

There was a muffled cry from outside, as Enzo tried to get the thing out.

"Drone down!" Rocco said.

"Time to finish him off!" Jagger replied.

Our next move was to line the drones up, hovering with menace in the air a few metres away from Enzo. He looked up at them with fear in his eyes.

"Ohhhhh noooooooo!" we heard him cry.

All at once, we shot the line of drones forward so they were hurtling towards him. He ran forwards, right into their path, and tried to duck down, but he was too slow; we swooped, crashing them all right into him. He lost balance and smacked down right into the gravel, skidding along with the force. We all sucked in breath over our teeth as we winced. "Oooh, gravel cuts *hurt!*" I said. "He's gonna need a big *Elastoplast* for that!"

"He's retreating!" Jagger shouted.

We all ran outside, as Enzo scrambled up and ran away, up the drive, back to his van.

"Come on!" Chloe screamed.

We hurtled up the path, desperate to catch him

before he had a chance to escape in his van.

We needn't have worried.

Enzo was kicking his van in frustration when we caught up with him. There was a yellow ticket on the windscreen and one of the wheels had been clamped. *Good old Mum!* I remembered there were traffic restrictions on this road – it was why mum couldn't park the car and we had to end up walking to Rocco's – and now she'd only gone and slapped Enzo with a parking violation, making sure this master criminal wasn't going anywhere!

Tiana led the charge up to Enzo. "I know some basic self-defence moves, so are you going to make this easy, or hard?"

Enzo's face clouded over – he clearly wasn't ready

to give up yet!

"Fine," Tiana shrugged, administering a short chop to Enzo's back with her hand.

Enzo collapsed face-down into the gutter, while Rocco and Chloe tied him up with a large *Happy 11th Birthday!* banner they'd brought from the house.

We weren't taking any risks. We frog-marched a weak and limp Enzo into Rocco's back garden, where we strapped him into the "Terminator" fairground ride.

"Have a nice trip!" Rocco grinned. He turned to Jagger. "Turn it up to *maximum!*"

With that, we stood back as Jagger turned the dial on the ride, and Enzo was shot right up into the air, then dropped back down again, over, and over, and over, while Chloe called the police and told them to get here as fast as they could.

"He's definitely gonna lose his lunch," I mused, watching Enzo be flung about in the sky as he moaned and groaned.

"Now that," Jagger said, "is what I call teamwork!"

CHAPTER 27
THE DORK FORCE

Enzo was looking pretty green by the time the police arrived and carted him away, but he had been on the Terminator for about half an hour by that point. We all had to give statements to a woman called WPC Munroe, telling her exactly what had happened and how we pieced the mystery together. I won't lie, I was hopeful that there would be some sort of reward, since we'd basically cracked a case involving multiple burglaries over two years. And I don't mean a doughnut each, or a shiny sticker. I was thinking hard cash.

But, as it turned out, we got a sticker.

Rocco wouldn't wear his because the colour didn't

match his sailor outfit. They made us pose for a photo for the local newspaper. I hope the article is respectful, and makes us look like heroes, rather than a bunch of idiots wearing *Future Cop* stickers designed for five-year-olds.

Meanwhile, Mr and Mrs Rococo were laughing with Mum in their kitchen, enjoying her stories of parking violations and grateful that her quick thinking in clamping Enzo's van had helped thwart the crime. Apparently, she *did* tell Rocco's dad that she could "forget" about his SUV being parked on double yellows if me and Jagger got an invite to the party – which is *wild* and made me realize that there was one thing more important to Mum than her job: *me*.

But the mess wasn't quite sorted out, of course. A couple of things still remained. For a start, we were technically still hypnotized. When we explained this to the police, they all thought it was highly amusing, and spent fifteen whole minutes shouting the trigger words while we squawked, sniffed and needed to pee, but no one seemed to think being hypnotized like that was a problem for our futures. I mean, *adults*! What is the point of them? So there was that. And there was also the small matter of the cherub with the missing winkle, whom the police said we should return to the witch (even though they used the name "Sally Hopkins"). They said that they were sure she wasn't a witch, and she would understand.

But it was very obvious they were as scared of her as we were and didn't want to get involved.

We all headed back into the marquee so I could collect my stuff to give to Mum, and then the plan was for us all to go to Sally's and hope she didn't boil our bones in her cauldron.

"Well, would you look at that!" Rocco beamed as we walked into the marquee. "Ha!" He put his hand into the melting ice sculpture of the unicorn doing a handstand that was in front of him, broke away some of the ice, and pulled out a small concrete-looking object, which he held triumphantly aloft. "IT'S THE MISSING WINKLE!"

"How did it get there?!" I said.

"I don't know, but I'm guessing one of us must

have remembered Mr Banerjee's lesson from Friday afternoon, when he told us that we should pack a severed limb in ice until it can be reattached! When the cherub's winkle fell off, we obviously did the right thing and kept it on ice!"

No doubt about it, we were geniuses!

A few dabs of superglue later, and the peeing cherub was reunited with his winkle. Never mind Future Cops, we were Future Winkle Doctors!

Despite our jubilation, we were pretty nervous by the time we reached Sally's house. Luckily Jagger agreed to do the talking.

"We found your peeing cherub," he explained, plainly, when Sally answered her door. "He's had an accident with his winkle. He's better now, but you probably need to be careful." Jagger bundled the cherub into Sally's hands. "Thank you, miss, and good day to you."

Sally gasped, tears welling in her eyes. She seemed pretty choked up as we all walked away.

"Wait!" Sally said. We all turned back, and she narrowed her eyes at us. "Can I offer you all ... a reward?"

"It's a trap!" I whispered at Rocco. "It'll be a poisoned

apple or gingerbread. Always beware gingerbread!"

"I've got some Haribo in my—"

"Ooh, lovely, yes please!" we all chorused, following her inside her house like we'd never had a lesson about stranger danger.

"I love Hariboo," Rocco said.

"What did you call it?" I asked.

"Hariboo."

"Hari*boo*? Why are you saying Hari*boo*? It's *bo*! Hari-*bo!*"

"Hari-*boo*."

"You're weird."

Rocco shrugged. "Maybe we're *all* weird, we just don't know it. Oooh. Very philosophical!"

It turned out that Sally the Witch was (a) actually really nice and (b) not a witch at all, but a "spiritualist healer" (which I think means someone who walks barefoot around the garden a lot).

We explained to Sally what had really happened, and rather than being cross and disappointed with us, she not only said she understood, but that she could get rid of the hypnosis for us! She said a lot of adults wouldn't take our plight seriously, and that she knew all about how frustrating that was, since a lot of people said her magical healing crystals were "nonsense" too.

Sally sat us all down in a circle, holding hands, while she performed something called a "cleansing ritual" on us, which involved a lot of chanting, burning of some dried herbs, and finally sprinkling some magical water on our faces, which Sally said had come from the "spring of eternal life" but which I'm pretty sure I saw her get out her tap in the kitchen. It didn't matter though, because the ritual worked! We tested the trigger words afterwards, and none of us reacted. Finally! We were free! It really was all over.

As we walked back to Rocco's, we bumped into Posh Chloe and Sporty Chloe.

"Rocco, we were looking for you!" Posh Chloe said, totally ignoring the rest of us. "Your mum said that everything has been sorted out now, so we wondered if you wanted to come round for a pamper-and-movie night?"

"We're going to watch *Mean Girls*," Sporty Chloe added.

Posh Chloe nodded and clasped her hands together in glee. "It's so inspirational!"

Rocco chewed his lip. "I do like that film."

My heart sank. After everything we'd been through, and all Rocco's words about friendship, he was going to go back to hanging out with them.

"Exactly!" Posh Chloe beamed. "Just what you need after the day you've had!"

Rocco took a deep breath. "But I don't want to hang out with you."

Posh Chloe frowned. "You have other plans?"

"Yeah," Rocco nodded. "I'm having my own pamper party and maybe watch the *LEGO* movie." He glanced at all of us. "With my ... friends."

There was a moment of shocked silence, and then Posh Chloe laughed, scornfully. "Lego movie? Oh, that's very funny, Rocco. We'll see you at six, yeah?"

"No," Rocco said. "No, you won't see me. Because I'll be with Otis, Jagger, Tiana and *Fun* Chloe."

Posh Chloe's face turned from disbelief to hatred, her lip curling into a snarl. "Have you lost your mind, Rocco? You're going to hang out with these ... these *losers?* The Dork Patrol? You're going to nerd it up at Dweeb Central, are you?"

"Yes!" Rocco said. "Know why? *Because that's what I am!* I am a dork! And I like hanging out at Dweeb Central! I don't have to pretend with this lot. I can just be me, and I like being me. I like having fun, and laughing, and messing about and just being a kid, because we won't be kids for much longer! And I like having friends who will always be there for me, even when things sometimes go wrong, or bad. That's what a real friend is, Chloe! A real friend doesn't just run off at the first sign of trouble. They're by your side. *Always.*"

Posh Chloe snorted. "OK, whatever, Rocco. Can't wait to see how long you last when we *finally* get to secondary school." She shook her head, like he was a lost cause then thumped her chest with her fist. *"Rocco est Dorkus!"*

Rocco dropped his eyes to the ground. I knew he was as worried about secondary school as the rest of us. But I also knew that, together, we would be just fine. Together, no one could touch us. If we could defeat Enzo, secondary school would be a piece of cake.

I stepped forwards and put my hand on Rocco's shoulder. "Rocco doesn't need to worry about any of that," I said. "We may be dorks, but we're invincible dorks, we're—"

"The Dork Force!" Rocco declared.

I winced. "I was going to say, 'We're not worried about secondary school because we have each other'? You know, something *moving*? But, sure, we're 'The Dork Force', because *that* won't get us beaten up. Jeez."

Rocco smiled. "Goodbye, the Chloes."

With that, he pushed past them, the rest of us following behind, and we headed back to his house.

Rocco fixed up some bowls of popcorn and nachos with melted cheese, guacamole and sour cream, and we all settled down in his cinema room. We weren't watching a regular movie, though. Mum had persuaded her mates at the council to let her have some of the CCTV footage from last night, so for the first time we were able to see exactly what we had got up to and how it all happened.

"Haha! Look at you!" Jagger howled, as we watched

the grainy footage of Chloe scale the wall at Sally's house, like some sort of cat-woman. She returned, moments later, holding the cherub, which she passed over the wall to Rocco, before clambering back over herself.

"Funny how I don't remember *any* of this!" Rocco said as he munched popcorn. "We were all on auto-pilot!"

The next clip showed me fishing Miss Percival's wedding dress out of the bin, ditching my own clothes (*why?!*), standing in the middle of the park in just my socks, trainers and boxers, before finally putting the dress on.

"Wow, you lot were really out of it!" Jagger laughed. He patted my leg. "But you looked great in that dress."

"Thanks!" I beamed. "I did feel special. I hope I get married one day. Which reminds me, I need to file for a divorce from Mark Longbottom. Ugh, so much admin! Or maybe I should get to know him before I make any final decisions?"

The footage snapped to a shot round the back of the theatre, where the four of us opened the stable door and got the donkey out; a shot from a camera on the high street showing Tiana leading the donkey along, and me *riding* it. Cut to: the church, where we find the crate of doves waiting for Miss Percival's wedding, which Tiana grabs.

"I hope those doves found their way home," Tiana said.

Rocco laughed. "Enzo told us to steal 'valuable' things, but I guess we didn't quite manage that!"

"It's open to interpretation!" I said. "The doves were valuable if you wanted them for your wedding. Maybe not otherwise."

"You realize while you were out creating all this mayhem, I was still hiding here?" Jagger said.

"How long were you there?" Chloe asked.

Jagger shrugged. "Dunno, I fell asleep at one point. Woke up, wasn't sure what time it was. Waited a bit longer. Oh, I needed a wee, so I..."

"Please tell me you went to the bathroom," Rocco said.

"I couldn't do that! I might have blown my hiding place and lost at Sardines!" Jagger said, looking outraged. "There was a handy metal cup thing in the cupboard I was in."

Rocco paused the video. "Metal cup thing? Hang on, you don't mean the goblet of eternal life that came from the archaeological dig in Egypt?"

Jagger shrugged. "Dunno. I guess it looked pretty old."

"Pretty old?! It's over *two thousand years old*! It's said to possess magical properties, gifting eternal life to all who sup from it!"

"What about all who *pee* in it?" Jagger asked.

"I've no idea! You've probably unleashed a curse!" Rocco said. "You actually peed in the goblet of eternal life?! Ahhhhh, man!"

We were all silent for a moment.

"Oh, um ... well, sorry, Rocco. I didn't know," Jagger said.

Rocco burst out laughing. "I'm kidding! Of course it's not the goblet of eternal life, what do you think I am?! It's probably just one of the stupid trophies Dad won for golf. I think we can forgive you, especially since you took on Enzo."

Jagger grinned. "I heard this weird scraping noise,

and then a window being forced open," he said. "I knew something wasn't right, and when I saw this weird guy creeping about, I knew I had to do something." He shrugged. "So I snuck around and collected up some stuff that I hoped I'd be able to use to stop him."

"I'm very grateful for what you did," Rocco said. "I'm grateful to you all. Thank you for helping me. Thank you for … yeah."

"I'm glad we all found each other eventually," I said. "And I don't know about any of you, but I feel like we could take on the world right now!"

"Or at least survive year seven at Grimstone High!" Tiana grinned.

"To us!" I said, raising a cup of warm Ribena. "To the Dork Force!"

"THE DORK FORCE!" everyone chorused.

I smiled, because I'd finally found my people. I'd always be mates with Jagger, but now I had more friends, and I realized an important thing that day: the people you're looking for are probably right under your nose, hiding in plain sight. You've just got to give them a chance.

EPILOGUE

I NEED TO PEE! AGAIN!

I woke up the following morning relieved to be in my own bed. What a weekend! I wouldn't normally be super happy about school on a Monday, but I was looking forward to a bit of normality.

We'd finished watching the rest of the CCTV footage at Rocco's. I laughed aloud to myself, suddenly remembering the winkle. (There had been a great shot of a massive dog biting it off the cherub – the crazed dog had been after the sausages.) Then I stretched and yawned, still smiling. "Dork Force," I muttered, chuckling. Then—

"AAAARRRRRHHHHHHH!"

I sat up in bed. Mum! Screaming! In the garden!

"AAAAAARHHHHHHHHHHHHHHH! ARGH!
AAAAAAAAHHHHHH!"

I leaped out of bed, lunged over to my window,
threw the curtains open and—

I froze.

Outside.

In my garden.

Oh no, no, no, no, no!

Three sheep. Spray-painted

pink.

Ten traffic cones.

A collection of giant vegetables – a marrow, some
onions, possibly some kind of parsnip.

A huge pile of giant underpants.

A supermarket trolley ... full of cheese.

And in the middle of it all, snapping away... Was that
a CROCODILE?

I swallowed, blinked, rubbed my eyes to try and make it all go away, because this was a dream, right? I was dreaming, this couldn't be … real?

No. It was real.

Had it happened again? How?!

My bedroom door flew open. Mum stood there, hands on hips, glowering at me. "Otis!" she bellowed. *"What is going on?!"*

I stared at her, trembling. Then my hand flew up in the air.

"I NEED TO PEE!"

DORK PATROL

Written by John Burger

A master criminal is behind bars tonight thanks to some super-sleuthing by a gang of pint-sized detectives. <u>Self-proclaimed</u> "Sausage King" Otis Mumble (11) led the

group of titchy Sherlocks as they pieced together the clues that put an end to a string of burglaries that had the police baffled.

"We can't wait to get to secondary school, when we'll be on the lookout for more crimes to solve – so watch

Not "self-proclaimed" – I actually am!

Not my name!

Is this a dig at my height?

I categorically did NOT say this!

out, big kids!" squeaky-voiced Otis Fumble (who is 133 cm tall) told our reporter.

OK, we get it, I'm short!

is feels liberated now!

"We have NO FEAR about grassing up a year nine, if necessary!" added fellow wannabe cop, Rococococococococo. "Who wants some?!"

Kid's got a death wish!

enough, name is to spell

The plucky little investigators were proud to receive some special stickers from the local police force to reward them for their quick thinking. "Who doesn't love to be made to look really bad at their job by a group of kids?" commented Detective Inspector Samson.

"We're the Dork Force!" said crime-fighting squad member, Jagger Jung (11 and 1/4).

"Please don't print that!" Otis Bummel joked. "We're going to get our heads kicked in at secondary school in September!"

Wasn't a joke, actually begged them

One thing's for sure: this pre-teen *Scooby* gang have plenty more mysteries to solve. In fact, the town mayor has offered a reward for information about a boy "of diminutive stature" who she caught urinating in the prize flower beds on Sunday afternoon.

Oh, boy!

ACKNOWLEDGEMENTS

A huge, massive THANK YOU to the team who helped to get *Sleepover Takeover* into your hands today!

Aleksei Bitskoff – I won't ever stop being wowed by your brilliant illustrations and your incredible talent at somehow managing to capture exactly what is in my head, even when it's super ridiculous!

My editor, Linas Alsenas, thank you for letting me loose on another zany story, for championing it, and for all your notes and advice on making it better … and even more zany! Working with you is always a dream, always a good laugh, and I'm so lucky.

The amazing team at Scholastic UK, who are so hard-working, talented, and passionate, including my brilliant publicist, Harriet Dunlea, marketing guru Ella Probert, and fabulous designer Liam Drane, as well as the Sales and Rights teams and all the lovely reps from Bounce. Big thanks also to Sarah Dutton for your proofreading magnificence and to Pete Matthews – especially for your advice on fried chicken restaurants with potentially dodgy slogans!

Thanks to my agent, Joanna Moult at Skylark Literary, for all your support, advice and all the general merriment (and tales of dog naughtiness) during our phone calls!

To my own little squad – Sarah Counsell, Beau and Dolly – thank you – even if you do insist on continually chewing all the boxes in my office (that's Beau and Dolly, not Sarah), and to Mum, Jonathan, Liz, and Alfie, Tricia, and Sue and Peter Counsell.

I'd like to thank everyone who supported my debut

middle-grade, *Life of Riley*, and helped introduce me to younger readers, especially the gang at the Blue Peter Book Awards, BookTrust, and all the booksellers, librarians, teachers and bloggers who championed it.

This book is dedicated to the students of two primary schools who were my Book Pen Pals 2020–21. Suffice to say, it wasn't the easiest of years for any of us, but when life gets hard, I think two things can help get you through: laughter and friendship. Whatever life throws at you, remember it always feels good to laugh, remember you're never alone, and remember the people you need are often right there in front of you. Make sure you look out for one another at secondary school, folks.

Finally, thanks to YOU for picking up *Sleepover Takeover*! Hope you loved reading it as much as I loved writing it.

BWARK!

Simon x

Simon James Green is an award-winning author of books for children and young adults. His YA novels include *Noah Can't Even*, *Noah Could Never*, *Alex in Wonderland*, (nominated for the Carnegie medal), *Heartbreak Boys* and *You're the One That I Want*. Simon's picture books, *Llama Glamarama* and *Fabulous Frankie* are both illustrated by Garry Parsons. His first middle-grade novel, *Life of Riley: Beginner's Luck* was shortlisted for the Blue Peter Book Award.

You can find out more about Simon's books at www.simonjamesgreen.com or follow him on Twitter or Instagram: @simonjamesgreen.

Riley is cursed. No, really! After a fairground incident
– TOTALLY not his fault – bad luck follows Riley
everywhere, causing disaster after disaster. It's got so
bad that no one wants to go near Riley, including his
teachers! But when new student Brad Chicago shows
up, Riley quickly realizes that Brad is the human
equivalent of a good luck charm.